悅讀
莎士比亞
經典喜劇故事

作者_ Charles and Mary Lamb
譯者 _ Cosmos Language Workshop

馴悍記
終成眷屬
一報還一報
冬天的故事

目錄

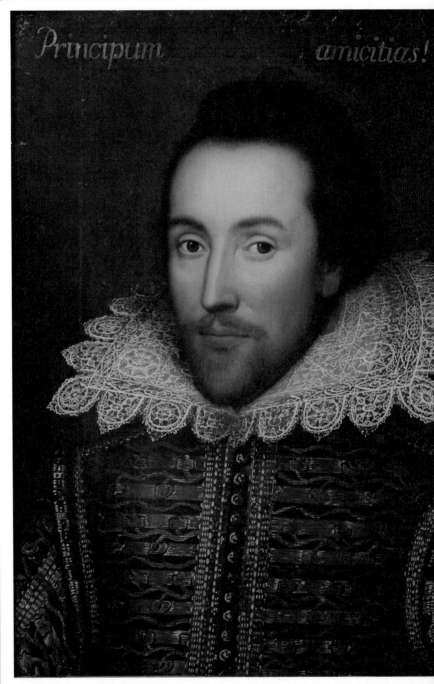

威廉·莎士比亞（William Shakespeare, 1564–1681）

莎士比亞二三事

威廉・莎士比亞（William Shakespeare）出生於英國的史特拉福（Stratford-upon-Avon）。莎士比亞的父親曾任地方議員，母親是地主的女兒。莎士比亞對婦女在廚房或起居室裡勞動的描繪不少，這大概是經由觀察母親所得。他本人也懂得園藝，故作品中的植草種樹表現鮮活。

1571 年，莎士比亞進入公立學校就讀，校內教學多採拉丁文，因此在其作品中到處可見到羅馬詩人奧維德（Ovid）的影子。當時代古典文學的英譯日漸普遍，有學者認為莎士比亞只懂得英語，但這種說法有可議之處。舉例來說，在高登的譯本裡，森林女神只用 Diana 這個名字，而莎士比亞卻在《仲夏夜之夢》一劇中用奧維德原作中的 Titania 一名來稱呼仙后。和莎士比亞有私交的文學家班・強生（Ben Jonson）則曾說，莎翁「懂得一點拉丁文，和一點點希臘文」。

莎士比亞的劇本亦常引用《聖經》典故，在伊麗莎白女王時期，通俗英語中已有很多《聖經》詞語。此外，莎士比亞應該很知悉當時年輕人所流行的遊戲娛樂，當時也應該有巡迴劇團不時前來史特拉福演出。 1575 年，伊麗莎白女王來到郡上時，當地人以化裝遊行、假面戲劇、煙火來款待女王，《仲夏夜之夢》裡就有這種盛會的描繪。

莎士比亞出生地：史特拉福（Stratford-upon-Avon）

環球劇場（Globe Theatre）（1997 年重建）

1582 年，莎士比亞與安・海瑟威（Anne Hathaway）結婚，但
這場婚姻顯得草率，連莎士比亞的雙親都因不知情而沒有出席
婚禮。1586 年，他們在倫敦定居下來。1586 年的倫敦已是英
國首都，年輕人莫不想在此大展抱負。史特拉福與倫敦之間的
交通頻仍，但對身無長物的人而言，步行仍是最平常的旅行方
式。伊麗莎白時期的文學家喜好步行，1618 年，班・強生就曾
在倫敦與愛丁堡之間徒步來回。

莎士比亞初抵倫敦的史料不充足，有諸多揣測。其中一說為莎
士比亞曾在律師處當職員，因為他在劇本與詩歌中經常提及法
律術語。但這種說法站不住腳，因為莎士比亞多有訛用，例如
他在《威尼斯商人》和《一報還一報》中提到的法律原理和程
序，就有諸多錯誤。事實上，伊麗莎白時期的作家都喜歡引用
法律詞彙，這是因為當時的文人和律師時有往來，而且中產階
級也常介入訴訟案件，許多法律術語自然為常人所知。莎士比
亞樂於援用法律術語，這顯示了他對當代生活和風尚的興趣。
莎士比亞自抵達倫敦到告老還鄉，心思始終放在戲劇和詩歌
上，不太可能接受法律這門專業領域的訓練。

莎士比亞在倫敦的第一份工作是劇場工作。當時常態營業的劇
場有兩個：「劇場」（the Theatre）和「帷幕」（the Curtain）。
「劇場」的所有人為詹姆士・波比奇（James Burbage），莎士
比亞就在此落腳。「劇場」財務狀況不佳，1596 年波比奇過
世，把「劇場」交給兩個兒子，其中一個兒子便是著名的悲劇
演員理查・波比奇（Richard Burbage）。後來「劇場」因租約
問題無法解決，決定將原有的建築物拆除，在泰晤士河的對面
重建，改名為「環球」（the Globe）。不久，「環球」就展開了
戲劇史上空前繁榮的時代。

伊麗莎白時期的戲劇表演只有男演員，所有的女性角色都由男性擔任。演員反串時會戴上面具，效果十足，不損故事的意境。莎士比亞本身也是一位出色的演員，曾在《皆大歡喜》和《哈姆雷特》中分別扮演忠僕亞當和國王鬼魂這兩個角色。

莎士比亞很留意演員的說白，這點可從哈姆雷特告誡伶人的對話中窺知一二。莎士比亞熟稔劇場的技術與運作，加上他也是劇場股東，故對劇場的營運和組織都甚有研究。不過，他的志業不在演出或劇場管理，而是劇本和詩歌創作。

1591 年，莎士比亞開始創作戲劇，他師法擅長喜劇的約翰・李利（John Lyly），以及曾寫下轟動一時的悲劇《帖木兒大帝》（*Tamburlaine the Great*）的克里斯多夫・馬婁（Christopher Marlowe）。莎翁戲劇的特色是兼容並蓄，吸收各家長處，而且他也勤奮多產。一直到 1611 年封筆之前，每年平均寫出兩部劇作和三卷詩作。莎士比亞慣於在既有的文學作品中尋找材料，又重視大眾喜好，常能讓平淡無奇的作品廣受喜愛。

在當時，劇本都是賣斷給劇場，不能再賣給出版商，因此莎劇的出版先後，並不能反映其創作的時間先後。莎翁作品的先後順序都由後人所推斷，推測的主要依據是作品題材和韻格。他早期的戲劇作品，無論悲劇或喜劇，性質都很單純。隨著創作的手法逐漸成熟，內容愈來愈複雜深刻，悲喜劇熔冶一爐。

自 1591 年席德尼爵士（Sir Philip Sidney）的十四行詩集發表後，十四行詩（sonnets，另譯為商籟）在英國即普遍受到文人的喜愛與仿傚。其中許多作品承續佩脫拉克（Petrarch）的風格，多描寫愛情的酸甜苦樂。莎士比亞的創作一向很能反應當時的文學風尚，在詩歌體裁鼎盛之時，他也將才華展現在十四行詩上，並將部分作品寫入劇本之中。

莎士比亞的十四行詩主要有兩個主題：婚姻責任和詩歌的不朽。這兩者皆是文藝復興時期詩歌中常見的主題。不少人以為莎士比亞的十四行詩表達了他個人的自省與懺悔，但事實上這些內容有更多是源於他的戲劇天分。

1595 至 1598 年，莎士比亞陸續寫了《羅密歐與茱麗葉》、《仲夏夜之夢》、《馴悍記》、《威尼斯商人》和若干歷史劇，他的詩歌戲劇也在這段時期受到肯定。當時的法蘭西斯・梅爾斯（Francis Meres）就將莎士比亞視為最偉大的文學家，他說：「要是繆思會說英語，一定也會喜歡引用莎士比亞的精彩語藻。」「無論是悲劇或喜劇，莎士比亞的表現都是首屈一指。」

闊別故鄉十一年後，莎士比亞於 1596 年返回故居，並在隔年買下名為「新居」（New Place）的房子。那是鎮上第二大的房子，他大幅改建整修，爾後家道日益興盛。莎士比亞大筆的固定收入主要來自表演，而非劇本創作。當時不乏有成功的演員靠演戲發財，甚至有人將這種現象寫成劇本。除了表演，劇場行政和管理的工作，以及宮廷演出的賞賜，都是他的財源。許多文獻均顯示，莎士比亞是個非常關心財富、地產和社會地位的人，讓許多人感到與他的詩人形象有些扞格不入。

伊麗莎白女王過世後，詹姆士一世（James I）於 1603 年登基，他把莎士比亞所屬的劇團納入保護。莎士比亞此時寫了《第十二夜》和佳評如潮的《哈姆雷特》，成就傲視全英格蘭。但他仍謙恭有禮、溫文爾雅，一如十多前年初抵倫敦的樣子，因此也愈發受到大眾的喜愛。

史特拉福聖三一教堂（Holy Trinity Church）
的莎翁紀念雕像和莎翁之墓

從這一年起，莎士比亞開始撰寫悲劇《奧賽羅》。他寫悲劇並非是因為精神壓力或生活變故，而是身為一名劇作家，最終目的就是要寫出優秀的悲劇作品。當時他嘗試以詩入劇，在《哈姆雷特》和《一報還一報》中尤其爐火純青。隨後《李爾王》和《馬克白》問世，一直到四年後的《安東尼與克麗奧佩脫拉》，寫作風格登峰造極。

1609 年，倫敦瘟疫猖獗，隔年，莎士比亞決定告別倫敦，返回史特拉福退隱。1616 年，莎士比亞和老友德雷頓、班·強生聚會時，可能由於喝得過於盡興，回家後發高熱，一病不起。他將遺囑修改完畢後，恰巧在他 52 歲的生日當天去世。

七年後，昔日的劇場友人收錄他的劇本做為全集出版，包括喜劇、歷史劇、悲劇等共 36 部。此書不僅不負莎翁本人所託，也為後人留下珍貴而豐富的文化資源，其中不僅包括美妙動人的詞句，還有各種人物的性格塑造與著墨。

除了作品，莎士比亞本人也在生前受到讚揚。班·強生曾說他是個「正人君子，天性開放自由，想像力出奇，擁有大無畏的思想，言詞溫和，蘊含機智」。也有學者以勇敢、敏感、平衡、幽默和身心健康這五種特質來形容莎士比亞，並說他「將無私的愛奉為至上，認為罪惡的根源是恐懼，而非金錢。」

因為這些劇本刻畫入微，具有知性，有人認為不可能是未受過大學教育的莎士比亞所作，因而引發爭議。有人推測出真正的作者，其中較為人所知的有法蘭西斯·培根（Francis Bacon）和牛津的德維爾公爵（Edward de Vere of Oxford），後者形成了頗具影響力的牛津學派。儘管傳說繪聲繪影，各種假說和研究不斷，但大概沒有人會說莎士比亞是虛構人物。

左：姊姊瑪麗（Mary Lamb, 1764–1847）
右：弟弟查爾斯（Charles Lamb, 1775–1834）

作者簡介：蘭姆姊弟

姊姊瑪麗（Mary Lamb）生於 1764 年，弟弟查爾斯（Charles Lamb）於 1775 年也在倫敦呱呱落地。因為家境不夠寬裕，瑪麗沒有接受過完整的教育。她從小就做針線活，幫忙持家，照顧母親。查爾斯在學生時代結識了詩人柯立芝（Samuel Taylor Coleridge），兩人成為終生的朋友。查爾斯後來因家中經濟困難而輟學， 1792 年轉而就職於東印度公司（East India House），這是他謀生的終身職業。

查爾斯在二十歲時一度精神崩潰，瑪麗則因為長年工作過量，在 1796 年突然精神病發，持刀攻擊父母，母親不幸傷重身亡。這件人倫悲劇發生後，瑪麗被判為精神異常，送往精神病院。查爾斯為此放棄自己原本期待的婚姻，以便全心照顧姊姊，使她免於在精神病院終老。

十九世紀的英國教育重視莎翁作品，一般的中產階級家庭也希望孩子早點接觸莎劇。 1806 年，文學家兼編輯高德溫（William Godwin）邀請查爾斯協助「少年圖書館」的出版計畫，請他將莎翁的劇本改寫為適合兒童閱讀的故事。

查爾斯接受這項工作後就與瑪麗合作，他負責六齣悲劇，瑪麗負責十四齣喜劇並撰寫前言。瑪麗在後來曾描述說，他們兩人

蘭姆姊弟的《莎士比亞故事集》(*Tales from Shakespeare*)
1922 年版的卷首插畫

「就坐在同一張桌子上改寫，看起來就好像《仲夏夜之夢》裡的荷米雅與海蓮娜一樣。」就這樣，姊弟兩人合力完成了這一系列的莎士比亞故事。《莎士比亞故事集》在 1807 年出版後便大受好評，建立了查爾斯的文學聲譽。

查爾斯的寫作風格獨特，筆法樸實，主題豐富。他將自己的一生，包括童年時代、基督教會學校的生活、東印度公司的光陰、與瑪麗相伴的點點滴滴，以及自己的白日夢、鍾愛的書籍和友人等等，都融入在文章裡，作品充滿細膩情感和豐富的想像力。他的軟弱、怪異、魅力、幽默、口吃，在在都使讀者感到親切熟悉，而獨特的筆法與敘事方式，也使他成為英國出色的散文大師。

1823 年，查爾斯和瑪麗領養了一個孤兒愛瑪。兩年後，查爾斯自東印度公司退休，獲得豐厚的退休金。查爾斯的健康情形和瑪麗的精神狀況卻每況愈下。 1833 年，愛瑪嫁給出版商後，又只剩下姊弟兩人。 1834 年 7 月，由於幼年時代的好友柯立芝去世，查爾斯的精神一蹶不振，沉湎酒精。此年秋天，查爾斯在散步時不慎跌倒，傷及顏面，後來傷口竟惡化至不可收拾的地步，而於年底過世。

查爾斯善與人交，和許多文人都保持良好情誼，又因為他一生對姊姊的照顧不餘遺力，所以也廣受敬佩。查爾斯和瑪麗兩人都終生未婚，查爾斯曾在一篇伊利亞小品中，將他們的狀況形容為「雙重單身」（double singleness）。查爾斯去世後，瑪麗的心理狀態雖然漸趨惡化，但一直到十三年後才辭世。

The Taming of the Shrew

馴悍記

《馴悍記》導讀

故事來源

《馴悍記》（ *The Taming of the Shrew* ）在 1623 年莎劇全集第一對開本（the First Folio）出版後才首次問世，此劇完成的年代推測可能在 1590–94 年間。但早在 1594 年，就有另一個名為《馴悍婦》（ *The Taming of a Shrew* ）的劇本印行，其基本架構與《馴悍記》相仿，只是內容較為粗糙。

這兩個劇本於是引起一番爭議：到底《馴悍婦》和《馴悍記》是不是同一個劇本？如果不是，作者是否都是莎士比亞？無獨有偶地，莎劇還有其他類似的情形，例如《冬天的故事》的原名 *The Winter's Tale* ，但也有人稱為 *A Winter's Tale* ；《連環錯》中 *The Comedy of Errors* ，偶爾也有人稱為 *A Comedy of Errors* 。這些爭議到目前為止仍沒有答案。

學者認為《馴悍婦》是其他劇作家仿《馴悍記》所寫成。在十六世紀，馴服悍婦的故事盛行於民間，當時所謂的悍婦，往往是指有主見或多言的婦女，而非充滿負面形象的潑辣女子。

當時，一般所認為的理想妻子乃是貞潔、寡言且順從。相反地，有主見或多言的婦女不僅不符合上述的條件，還會被認為是性生活不檢點。對於悍婦，一般多有懲戒，不僅讓她們無法開口說話，連她們的丈夫都可能因「管教不當」而遭連坐懲罰。

悍妻的主題

羅馬喜劇中時常可見刁鑽潑辣的妻子。在這個主題上，伊麗莎白時期的劇作家向普勞特斯（Plautus）和泰瑞斯（Terrence）取經，將他們的劇本改編為英語版本。除了劇本，十四世紀的英國詩人喬叟（Chaucer）也早就在著作中對這個主題貢獻良多，形成一股文學傳統。

《馴悍記》原劇由三條故事線組合而成，分別取材自不同來源。蘭姆改寫的這個版本僅取凱瑟琳和皮楚丘的故事，這是一般人在提到這個劇本時所描述的大綱。這條故事線的來源可能是 1550 年的英國民謠《快樂兒戲：用馬皮裹住狡獪該死的妻子教她舉止端正》（*A Merry Jest of a Shrewd and Curst Wife Lapped in Morel's Skin for Her Good Behaviour*）。雖名為「快樂兒戲」，丈夫的手段卻很野蠻，用不堪的方式對待妻子。

相較之下，皮楚丘的手段就堪稱聰明且符合人道精神，因為他並沒有真正使用暴力，就讓凱瑟琳的個性轉為溫和。《馴悍記》的場景設在義大利的鄉間，但是皮楚丘馴服凱瑟琳的手法卻很英式。他不像一般義大利人會用情歌和詩篇來追求心上人，而是用語言來壓制凱瑟琳。他也用英國男性的鐵腕來對待妻子，以確保自己的男性氣概。莎士比亞藉由此鮮明性格的對比，將英國男性與法、義等其他國家的男性加以區隔。

凱瑟琳脾氣暴躁,皮楚丘「以其人之道,還治其人之身」,甚至比她更加暴躁。他動輒發怒,冷熱無常,對馬匹、僕人、裁縫師大吼大叫,好讓她明白此種行徑多麼令人無法忍受。接著,他剝奪她的飲食睡眠,迫使她為求生存而克制原本潑悍的脾氣。其實皮楚丘並不是真的想控制凱瑟琳的身心,而是希望她能學習自制,為他人著想。

凱瑟琳最後歌頌「婦從夫意」的一席話,雖然有些誇張諷刺,但也意味了她對自我的正面認同。這種心理攻防的層面,也是《馴悍記》特出的一個原因。

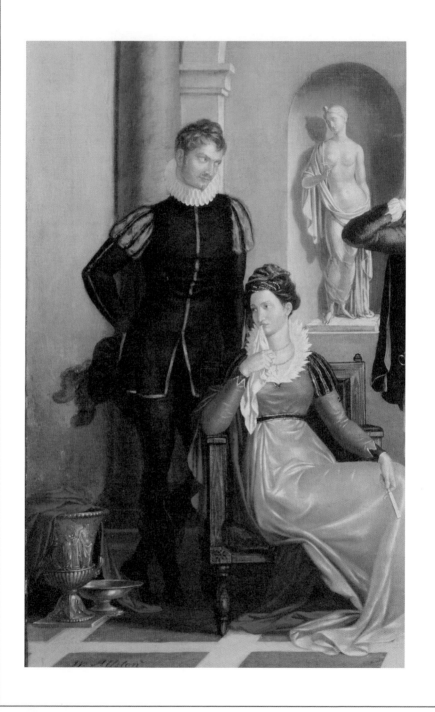

夫妻相處之道

其實，莎士比亞對女性的認同與了解，與當時的劇作家所抱持的觀點大不相同。他喜劇中的女性角色不但常常搶盡男性風采，還往往主宰劇情的走向，如《威尼斯商人》的鮑希雅、《皆大歡喜》的羅莎琳、《第十二夜》的菲兒拉等等。不過莎士比亞仍承襲了基督教中的尊夫思想，所以才會有凱瑟琳「倡導婦道」的那一段話。

在清教徒的傳統裡，丈夫不會對妻子使用暴力，而是把她視為精神伴侶和家務上的助手。在他們的眼中，婚姻不僅合乎經濟效益，而且也必須建立在互敬互愛的基礎上。對家庭的觀點，也有人持「家國論」，認為家庭就如同國家，丈夫是君王，妻小是臣民，倘若沒有明顯的階級劃分，國家就有崩塌的危險。若從這兩個觀點來看，《馴悍記》便很接近上述的兩種理論。

不少評論家都同意，皮楚丘和凱瑟琳這兩個角色深富人性、生氣和想像力，所作所為也教人信服。在這齣戲中，語言可說是支配、獲得權力的工具。凱瑟琳的嘴上工夫了得，被認為欠缺教養，皮楚丘就利用言語反制她，讓她隨他的意思指鹿為馬。

也有不少人認為，他們兩人之間不單純是馴妻，而是像《無事生非》裡的碧翠絲和班狄克一樣，都是不罵不相識的歡喜冤家，代表某種類型的愛情故事。一般在演出時，除非是刻意要醜化角色，否則皮楚丘都對凱瑟琳情深意重。

這齣劇有著兩性戰爭的意味，皮楚丘最初是看上凱瑟琳的財產才娶她為妻，但兩人交手後，才發覺她個性十足，而他們的婚姻也代表了發現自我和互相了解的過程。

劇本的各種演出版本

《馴悍記》雖然有部分接近笑劇，但是劇情發展新奇、機智、有活力，在舞台上無論是演出全本、改編或是刪減版，向來都受到好評。十八世紀時，這個劇本就已經有七種不同的版本了，當中非常知名的就是 1754 年英國演員及劇作家蓋瑞克（David Garrick）的版本，他和改編本劇的作者蘭姆一樣，只保留凱瑟琳和皮楚丘這一段，劇名就叫做《凱瑟琳與皮楚丘》（*Catharine and Petruchio*）。

另外，在十八、十九世紀的演出中，皮楚丘也常常帶著皮鞭，當作制伏妻子與奴僕的象徵。二十世紀最有名的版本，就應屬理查·波頓與伊莉莎白·泰勒所擔綱演出的電影了。

「馴服女人」這種主題讓許多現代人不以為然，其實早在 1611 年，弗萊撤（John Fletcher）就曾經為女人喉舌，寫過《馴悍記》的續集《女人的獎品》（*The Woman's Prize, or The Tamer Tamed*）。劇中描述皮楚丘不斷遭到第二任妻子瑪莉亞的奚落與羞辱，在歷經四幕的發展之後，才因妻子自願遵守婦德，而恢復其男性的自尊。

現代有許多《馴悍記》的導演也會刪減凱瑟琳對皮楚丘的臣服，並將凱瑟琳遭受的不平待遇低調處理，有的導演甚至在凱瑟琳最後的一番話中，暗示她對那段話並非真正地心悅誠服。這些改編都得以「拯救」莎士比亞，使他免於被冠上男性沙文主義的封號。

《馴悍記》人物表

Katharine	凱瑟琳	一位富紳的大女兒，脾氣暴躁
Petruchio	皮楚丘	凱瑟琳的丈夫
Baptista	巴提塔	富紳，凱瑟琳之父
Bianca	碧安卡	凱瑟琳的妹妹
Lucentio	盧森修	碧安卡的丈夫
Vincentio	文森修	盧森修的父親
Hortensio	何天修	盧森修的友人

The Taming of the Shrew

Katharine, the Shrew[1], was the eldest daughter of Baptista, a rich gentleman of Padua. She was a lady of such an ungovernable spirit and fiery temper, such a loud-tongued scold[2], that she was known in Padua by no other name than Katharine the Shrew.

It seemed very unlikely, indeed impossible, that any gentleman would ever be found who would venture to marry this lady, and therefore Baptista was much blamed for deferring[3] his consent to many excellent offers that were made to her gentle sister Bianca, putting off all Bianca's suitors with this excuse that when the eldest sister was fairly off his hands, they should have free leave to address young Bianca.

1 shrew [ʃruː] (n.) 悍婦
2 scold [skoʊld] (n.) 好罵人者
3 defer [dɪˈfɜːr] (v.) 延緩

Katherine

It happened, however, that a gentleman, named Petruchio, came to Padua, purposely to look out for a wife, who, nothing discouraged by these reports of Katharine's temper, and hearing she was rich and handsome, resolved upon marrying this famous termagant[4], and taming her into a meek and manageable wife.

And truly none was so fit to set about this herculean[5] labour as Petruchio, whose spirit was as high as Katharine's, and he was a witty and most happy-tempered humourist, and withal[6] so wise, and of such a true judgment, that he well knew how to feign[7] a passionate and furious deportment[8], when his spirits were so calm that himself could have laughed merrily at his own angry feigning, for his natural temper was careless and easy.

The boisterous[9] airs he assumed[10] when he became the husband of Katharine being but in sport, or more properly speaking, affected by his excellent discernment[11], as the only means to overcome, in her own way, the passionate ways of the furious Katharine.

---

4 termagant ['tɜːrməgənt] (n.) 好爭吵的女子;悍婦
5 herculean [ˌhɜːr'kjuːliːən] (a.) 艱巨的;需要體力或智力的
6 withal [wɪ'ðɔːl] (adv.) 〔古代用法〕而且;此外

Petruchio

7 feign [feɪn] (v.) 假裝

8 deportment [dɪˈpɔːrtmənt] (n.) 行為；舉止

9 boisterous [ˈbɔɪstərəs] (a.) 喧鬧的

10 assume [əˈsuːm] (v.) 假裝；裝出

11 discernment [dɪˈsɜːrnmənt] (n.) 判斷力；明辨力

A courting then Petruchio went to Katharine the Shrew; and first of all he applied to Baptista her father, for leave to woo[12] his *gentle daughter* Katharine, as Petruchio called her, saying archly[13], that having heard of her bashful[14] modesty and mild behaviour, he had come from Verona to solicit[15] her love.

Her father, though he wished her married, was forced to confess Katharine would ill answer this character, it being soon apparent of what manner of gentleness she was composed, for her music-master rushed into the room to complain that the gentle Katharine, his pupil, had broken his head with her lute[16], for presuming[17] to find fault with her performance; which, when Petruchio heard, he said, "It is a brave wench[18]; I love her more than ever, and long to have some chat with her."

And hurrying the old gentleman for a positive answer, he said, "My business is in haste, Signior Baptista, I cannot come every day to woo. You knew my father: he is dead, and has left me heir to all his lands and goods. Then tell me, if I get your daughter's love, what dowry[19] you will give with her."

12 woo [wuː] (v.) 〔舊式用法〕追求；求婚

13 archly ['ɑːrtʃli] (adv.) 調皮地

14 bashful ['bæʃfəl] (a.) 害羞的

15 solicit [sə'lɪsɪt] (v.) 懇求

16 lute [luːt] (n.) 魯特琴   lute

17 presume [prɪ'zuːm] (v.) 敢於；擅敢

18 wench [wrentʃ] (n.) 〔古代用法〕少女；少婦

19 dowry ['daʊri] (n.) 嫁妝

Baptista thought his manner was somewhat blunt[20] for a lover; but being glad to get Katharine married, he answered that he would give her twenty thousand crowns for her dowry, and half his estate at his death: so this odd match was quickly agreed on, and Baptista went to apprise[21] his shrewish daughter of her lover's addresses, and sent her in to Petruchio to listen to his suit.

In the meantime Petruchio was settling with himself the mode of courtship he should pursue; and he said, "I will woo her with some spirit when she comes. If she rails[22] at me, why then I will tell her she sings as sweetly as a nightingale; and if she frowns[23], I will say she looks as clear as roses newly washed with dew. If she will not speak a word, I will praise the eloquence[24] of her language; and if she bids me leave her, I will give her thanks as if she bid[25] me stay with her a week."

Now the stately Katharine entered, and Petruchio first addressed her with "Good morrow, Kate, for that is your name, I hear."

20 blunt [blʌnt] (a.) 直言的;不客氣的

21 apprise [ə'praɪz] (v.)〔正式用法〕通知;報告

22 rail [reɪl] (v.)〔文學用法〕挑剔;抱怨

23 frown ['fraʊn] (v.) 皺眉頭

24 eloquence ['eləkwəns] (n.) 口才;雄辯

25 bid [bɪd] (v.) 說(問候的話等);邀請

🎧 **5** Katharine, not liking this plain salutation, said disdainfully[26], "They call me Katharine who do speak to me."

"You lie," replied the lover; "for you are called plain Kate, and bonny[27] Kate, and sometimes Kate the Shrew: but, Kate, you are the prettiest Kate in Christendom[28], and therefore, Kate, hearing your mildness praised in every town, I am come to woo you for my wife."

A strange courtship they made of it. She in loud and angry terms showing him how justly she had gained the name of Shrew, while he still praised her sweet and courteous words, till at length, hearing her father coming, he said (intending to make as quick a wooing as possible), "Sweet Katharine, let us set this idle chat aside, for your father has consented that you shall be my wife, your dowry is agreed on, and whether you will or no, I will marry you."

And now Baptista entering, Petruchio told him his daughter had received him kindly, and that she had promised to be married the next Sunday. This Katharine denied, saying she would rather see him hanged on Sunday, and reproached[29] her father for wishing to wed her to such a madcap ruffian[30] as Petruchio.

26 disdainfully [dɪsˈdeɪnfəli] (adv.) 輕蔑地
27 bonny [ˈbɑːni] (a.) 可愛的；美好的
28 Christendom [ˈkrɪsəndəm] (n.) 基督教世界
29 reproach [rɪˈproutʃ] (v.) 責備
30 ruffian [ˈrʌfiən] (n.) 惡棍；流氓

Petruchio desired her father not to regard her angry words, for they had agreed she should seem reluctant before him, but that when they were alone he had found her very fond and loving; and he said to her, "Give me your hand, Kate; I will go to Venice to buy you fine apparel[31] against our wedding day. Provide the feast, father, and bid the wedding guests. I will be sure to bring rings, fine array[32], and rich clothes, that my Katharine may be fine; and kiss me, Kate, for we will be married on Sunday."

On the Sunday all the wedding guests were assembled, but they waited long before Petruchio came, and Katharine wept for vexation[33] to think that Petruchio had only been making a jest of her.

At last, however, he appeared; but he brought none of the bridal finery[34] he had promised Katharine, nor was he dressed himself like a bridegroom, but in strange disordered attire[35], as if he meant to make a sport of the serious business he came about; and his servant and the very horses on which they rode were in like manner in mean and fantastic fashion habited.

31 apparel [ə'pærəl] (n.) 〔舊式用法〕〔文學用法〕衣服

32 array [ə'reɪ] (n.) 服裝

33 vexation [vek'seɪʃən] (n.) 苦惱

34 finery ['faɪnəri] (n.) 華麗的服裝

35 attire [ə'taɪr] (n.) 〔文學用法〕〔詩的用法〕服裝

7 Petruchio could not be persuaded to change his dress; he said Katharine was to be married to him, and not to his clothes; and finding it was in vain to argue with him, to the church they went, he still behaving in the same mad way, for when the priest asked Petruchio if Katharine should be his wife, he swore so loud that she should, that, all amazed, the priest let fall his book, and as he stooped[36] to take it up, this mad-brained bridegroom gave him such a cuff[37], that down fell the priest and his book again.

And all the while they were being married he stamped and swore so, that the high-spirited Katharine trembled and shook with fear. After the ceremony was over, while they were yet in the church, he called for wine, and drank a loud health to the company, and threw a sop[38] which was at the bottom of the glass full in the sexton's[39] face, giving no other reason for this strange act, than that the sexton's beard grew thin and hungerly, and seemed to ask the sop as he was drinking.

---

36 stoop [stuːp] (v.) 屈身；彎腰
37 cuff [kʌf] (n.) 掌擊；摑；打；拍
38 sop [sɑːp] (n.)（泡在牛奶、肉湯裡的）麵包片
39 sexton ['sekstən] (n.) 教堂司事

🎧 8 ▶ Never sure was there such a mad marriage; but Petruchio did but put this wildness on, the better to succeed in the plot he had formed to tame his shrewish wife.

Baptista had provided a sumptuous[40] marriage feast, but when they returned from church, Petruchio, taking hold of Katharine, declared his intention of carrying his wife home instantly: and no remonstrance[41] of his father-in-law, or angry words of the enraged Katharine, could make him change his purpose. He claimed a husband's right to dispose of his wife as he pleased, and away he hurried Katharine off: he seeming so daring and resolute that no one dared attempt to stop him.

Petruchio mounted his wife upon a miserable horse, lean and lank[42], which he had picked out for the purpose, and himself and his servant no better mounted; they journeyed on through rough and miry[43] ways, and ever when this horse of Katharine's stumbled, he would storm and swear at the poor jaded[44] beast, who could scarce crawl under his burthen[45], as if he had been the most passionate man alive.

40 sumptuous [ˈsʌmptʃuəs] (a.) 華麗的；奢侈的

41 remonstrance [rɪˈmɑːnstrəns] (n.) 抗議；規諫

42 lank [læŋk] (a.) 瘦長的

43 miry [ˈmaɪri] (a.) 泥濘的

44 jaded [ˈdʒeɪdɪd] (a.) 疲倦的

45 burthen [ˈbɜːrðən] (n.)〔文學用法〕負擔

At length, after a weary journey, during which Katharine had heard nothing but the wild ravings[46] of Petruchio at the servant and the horses, they arrived at his house.

Petruchio welcomed her kindly to her home, but he resolved she should have neither rest nor food that night. The tables were spread, and supper soon served; but Petruchio, pretending to find fault with every dish, threw the meat about the floor, and ordered the servants to remove it away; and all this he did, as he said, in love for his Katharine, that she might not eat meat that was not well dressed.

And when Katharine, weary and supperless, retired to rest, he found the same fault with the bed, throwing the pillows and bedclothes about the room, so that she was forced to sit down in a chair, where if she chanced to drop asleep, she was presently awakened by the loud voice of her husband, storming at the servants for the ill-making of his wife's bridal-bed.

The next day Petruchio pursued the same course, still speaking kind words to Katharine, but when she attempted to eat, finding fault with everything that

was set before her, throwing the breakfast on the floor as he had done the supper; and Katharine, the haughty[47] Katharine, was fain[48] to beg the servants would bring her secretly a morsel[49] of food; but they being instructed by Petruchio, replied, they dared not give her anything unknown to their master.

---

46 ravings ['reɪvɪŋz] (n.) 愚蠢或狂野的話
47 haughty ['hɔːti] (a.) 傲慢的
48 fain [feɪn] (a.) 〔詩的用法〕〔舊式用法〕不得不的；勉強的
49 morsel ['mɔːrsəl] (n.) 一小塊；一小片

🎧 10 "Ah," said she, "did he marry me to famish[50] me? Beggars that come to my father's door have food given them. But I, who never knew what it was to entreat for anything, am starved for want of food, giddy[51] for want of sleep, with oaths[52] kept waking, and with brawling[53] fed; and that which vexes me more than all, he does it under the name of perfect love, pretending that if I sleep or eat, it were present death to me."

Here the soliloquy[54] was interrupted by the entrance of Petruchio: he, not meaning she should be quite starved, had brought her a small portion of meat, and he said to her, "How fares[55] my sweet Kate? Here, love, you see how diligent I am, I have dressed your meat myself. I am sure this kindness merits thanks. What, not a word? Nay, then you love not the meat, and all the pains I have taken is to no purpose."

He then ordered the servant to take the dish away. Extreme hunger, which had abated[56] the pride of Katharine, made her say, though angered to the heart, "I pray you let it stand."

---

50 famish ['fæmɪʃ] (v.) 挨餓；飢餓
51 giddy ['gɪdi] (a.) 令人暈眩的
52 oath [ouθ] (n.) 詛咒
53 brawling ['brɔːlɪŋ] (n.) 吵鬧

54 soliloquy [sə'lɪləkwi] (n.) 自言自語

55 fare [fer] (v.) 過活；遭遇

56 abate [ə'beɪt] (v.)〔文學用法〕減少；減退

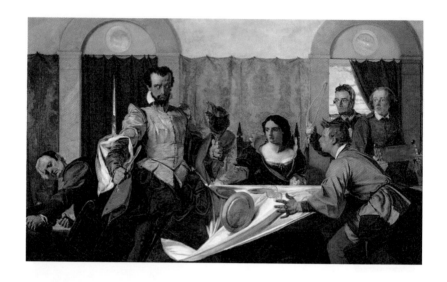

 But this was not all Petruchio intended to bring her to, and he replied, "The poorest service is repaid with thanks, and so shall mine before you touch the meat."

On this Katharine brought out a reluctant "I thank you, sir."

And now he suffered her to make a slender meal, saying, "Much good may it do your gentle heart, Kate; eat apace[57]! And now, my honey love, we will return to your father's house, and revel[58] it as bravely as the best, with silken coats and caps and golden rings, with ruffs[59] and scarfs and fans and double change of finery."

And to make her believe he really intended to give her these gay things, he called in a tailor and a haberdasher[60], who brought some new clothes he had ordered for her, and then giving her plate to the servant to take away, before she had half satisfied her hunger, he said, "What, have you dined?"

The haberdasher presented a cap, saying, "Here is the cap your worship bespoke;" on which Petruchio began to storm afresh, saying the cap was moulded in a porringer[61], and that it was no bigger than a cockle[62] or walnut shell, desiring the haberdasher to take it away and make it bigger.

Katharine said, "I will have this; all gentlewomen wear such caps as these."

"When you are gentle," replied Petruchio, "you shall have one too, and not till then."

ruff

57 apace [əˈpeɪs] (adv.) 〔舊代用法〕
〔文學用法〕急速地
58 revel [ˈrevəl] (v.) 狂歡享樂
59 ruff [rʌf] (n.) 十六世紀所戴的寬硬縐領
60 haberdasher [ˈhæbərdæʃər] (n.) 賣零星服飾、針線等的商人
61 porringer [ˈpɔːrɪndʒər] (n.) （小孩用的、有柄的）小湯碗
62 cockle [ˈkɑːkəl] (n.) 蛤蜊

The meat Katharine had eaten had a little revived her fallen spirits, and she said, "Why, sir, I trust I may have leave to speak, and speak I will: I am no child, no babe; your betters have endured to hear me say my mind; and if you cannot, you had better stop your ears."

Petruchio would not hear these angry words, for he had happily discovered a better way of managing his wife than keeping up a jangling[63] argument with her; therefore his answer was, "Why, you say true; it is a paltry[64] cap, and I love you for not liking it."

"Love me, or love me not," said Katharine, "I like the cap, and I will have this cap or none."

"You say you wish to see the gown," said Petruchio, still affecting[65] to misunderstand her.

The tailor then came forward and showed her a fine gown he had made for her. Petruchio, whose intent was that she should have neither cap nor gown, found as much fault with that.

"O mercy, heaven!" said he, "what stuff is here! What, do you call this a sleeve? it is like a demi-cannon, carved up and down like an apple tart."

The tailor said, "You bid me make it according to the fashion of the times;" and Katharine said, she never saw a better fashioned gown.

63 jangling ['dʒæŋglɪŋ] (a.) 吵鬧的
64 paltry ['pɔːltri] (a.) 不足取的；沒有價值的
65 affect [əˈfekt] (v.) 假裝

🎧 13 ▸ This was enough for Petruchio, and privately desiring these people might be paid for their goods, and excuses made to them for the seemingly strange treatment he bestowed upon them, he with fierce words and furious gestures drove the tailor and the haberdasher out of the room; and then, turning to Katharine, he said, "Well, come, my Kate, we will go to your father's even in these mean garments we now wear."

And then he ordered his horses, affirming they should reach Baptista's house by dinner-time, for that it was but seven o'clock. Now it was not early morning, but the very middle of the day, when he spoke this; therefore Katharine ventured to say, though modestly, being almost overcome by the vehemence[66] of his manner, "I dare assure you, sir, it is two o'clock, and will be supper-time before we get there."

But Petruchio meant that she should be so completely subdued[67], that she should assent[68] to everything he said, before he carried her to her father; and therefore, as if he were lord even of the sun, and could command the hours, he said it should be what time he pleased to have it, before he set forward; "For," he said, "whatever I say or do, you still are crossing it. I will not go today, and when I go, it shall be what o'clock I say it is."

66 vehemence [ˈviːəməns] (n.) 猛烈
67 subdued [səbˈduːd] (a.) 順從的
68 assent [əˈsent] (v.) 同意

Another day Katharine was forced to practise her newly-found obedience, and not till he had brought her proud spirit to such a perfect subjection, that she dared not remember there was such a word as contradiction, would Petruchio allow her to go to her father's house; and even while they were upon their journey thither[69], she was in danger of being turned back again, only because she happened to hint it was the sun, when he affirmed the moon shone brightly at noonday.

"Now, by my mother's son," said he, "and that is myself, it shall be the moon, or stars, or what I list, before I journey to your father's house."

He then made as if he were going back again; but Katharine, no longer Katharine the Shrew, but the obedient wife, said, "Let us go forward, I pray, now we have come so far, and it shall be the sun, or moon, or what you please, and if you please to call it a rush candle henceforth, I vow it shall be so for me."

This he was resolved to prove, therefore he said again, "I say, it is the moon."

"I know it is the moon," replied Katharine.

69 thither ['θɪðər] (adv.)〔舊式用法〕到那邊

"You lie, it is the blessed sun," said Petruchio.

"Then it is the blessed sun," replied Katharine; "but sun it is not, when you say it is not. What you will have it named, even so it is, and so it ever shall be for Katharine."

Now then he suffered her to proceed on her journey; but further to try if this yielding humour would last, he addressed an old gentleman they met on the road as if he had been a young woman, saying to him, "Good morrow, gentle mistress;" and asked Katharine if she had ever beheld[70] a fairer gentlewoman, praising the red and white of the old man's cheeks, and comparing his eyes to two bright stars; and again he addressed him, saying, "Fair lovely maid, once more good-day to you!" and said to his wife, "Sweet Kate, embrace her for her beauty's sake."

The now completely vanquished[71] Katharine quickly adopted her husband's opinion, and made her speech in like sort to the old gentleman, saying to him, "Young budding[72] virgin, you are fair, and fresh, and sweet: whither[73] are you going, and where is your dwelling? Happy are the parents of so fair a child."

"Why, how now, Kate," said Petruchio; "I hope you are not mad. This is a man, old and wrinkled, faded and withered, and not a maiden, as you say he is."

On this Katharine said, "Pardon me, old gentleman; the sun has so dazzled[74] my eyes, that everything I look on seemeth green. Now I perceive you are a reverend[75] father: I hope you will pardon me for my sad mistake."

"Do, good old grandsire," said Petruchio, "and tell us which way you are travelling. We shall be glad of your good company, if you are going our way."

The old gentleman replied, "Fair sir, and you, my merry mistress, your strange encounter has much amazed me. My name is Vincentio, and I am going to visit a son of mine who lives at Padua."

---

70 behold [bɪˈhoʊld] (v.)〔舊式用法〕〔文學用法〕看
71 vanquished [ˈvæŋkwɪʃt] (a.) 被征服的
72 budding [ˈbʌdɪŋ] (a.) 發芽的；開始發展的
73 whither [ˈwɪðər] (adv.)〔舊式用法〕往何處
74 dazzle [ˈdæzəl] (v.) 使眼花目眩
75 reverend [ˈrevərənd] (a.) 值得尊敬的

🎧 16 Then Petruchio knew the old gentleman to be the father of Lucentio, a young gentleman who was to be married to Baptista's younger daughter, Bianca, and he made Vincentio very happy, by telling him the rich marriage his son was about to make: and they all journeyed on pleasantly together till they came to Baptista's house, where there was a large company assembled to celebrate the wedding of Bianca and Lucentio, Baptista having willingly consented[76] to the marriage of Bianca when he had got Katharine off his hands.

When they entered, Baptista welcomed them to the wedding feast, and there was present also another newly married pair.

Lucentio, Bianca's husband, and Hortensio, the other new married man, could not forbear[77] sly jests, which seemed to hint at the shrewish disposition[78] of Petruchio's wife, and these fond bridegrooms seemed highly pleased with the mild tempers of the ladies they had chosen, laughing at Petruchio for his less fortunate choice.

Petruchio took little notice of their jokes till the ladies were retired after dinner, and then he perceived Baptista himself joined in the laugh against him: for when Petruchio affirmed that his wife would prove more obedient than theirs, the father of Katharine said, "Now, in good sadness, son Petruchio, I fear you have got the veriest shrew of all."

---

76 consent [kən'sɛnt] (v.) 同意
77 forbear ['fɔːrbɛr] (v.) 〔正式用法〕抑制
78 disposition [ˌdɪspə'zɪʃən] (n.) 性情；氣質

🎧 **17** "Well," said Petruchio, "I say no, and therefore for assurance that I speak the truth, let us each one send for his wife, and he whose wife is most obedient to come at first when she is sent for, shall win a wager[79] which we will propose."

To this the other two husbands willingly consented, for they were quite confident that their gentle wives would prove more obedient than the headstrong[80] Katharine; and they proposed a wager of twenty crowns, but Petruchio merrily said, he would lay as much as that upon his hawk or hound, but twenty times as much upon his wife.

Lucentio and Hortensio raised the wager to a hundred crowns, and Lucentio first sent his servant to desire Bianca would come to him. But the servant returned, and said, "Sir, my mistress sends you word she is busy and cannot come."

"How," said Petruchio, "does she say she is busy and cannot come? Is that an answer for a wife?"

---

79 wager ['weɪdʒər] (n.) 賭注
80 headstrong ['hedstrɔːŋ] (a.) 任性的；頑固的

Then they laughed at him, and said, it would be well if Katharine did not send him a worse answer.

And now it was Hortensio's turn to send for his wife; and he said to his servant, "Go, and entreat my wife to come to me."

"Oh ho! entreat her!" said Petruchio. "Nay, then, she needs must come."

"I am afraid, sir," said Hortensio, "your wife will not be entreated."

But presently this civil husband looked a little blank, when the servant returned without his mistress; and he said to him, "How now! Where is my wife?"

"Sir," said the servant, "my mistress says, you have some goodly jest in hand, and therefore she will not come. She bids you, come to her."

"Worse and worse!" said Petruchio; and then he sent his servant, saying, "Sirrah, go to your mistress, and tell her I command her to come to me."

The company had scarcely time to think she would not obey this summons, when Baptista, all in amaze, exclaimed, "Now, by my *holidame*, here comes Katharine!" and she entered, saying meekly[81] to Petruchio, "What is your will, sir, that you send for me?"

"Where is your sister and Hortensio's wife?" said he.

Katharine replied, "They sit conferring[82] by the parlor[83] fire."

"Go, fetch them hither!" said Petruchio.

Away went Katharine without reply to perform her husband's command.

"Here is a wonder," said Lucentio, "if you talk of a wonder."

"And so it is," said Hortensio; "I marvel what it bodes[84]."

"Marry, peace it bodes," said Petruchio, "and love, and quiet life, and right supremacy[85]; and, to be short, everything that is sweet and happy."

81 meekly ['miːkli] (adv.) 溫順地

82 confer [kənˈfɜːr] (v.) 商談；討論

83 parlor ['pɑːrlər] (n.) 客廳

84 bode [boʊd] (v.)〔舊時用法〕〔詩的用法〕預示

85 supremacy [suːˈpreməsi] (n.) 至高；無上

🎧 19 Katharine's father, overjoyed to see this reformation in his daughter, said, "Now, fair befall thee, son Petruchio! you have won the wager, and I will add another twenty thousand crowns to her dowry, as if she were another daughter, for she is changed as if she had never been."

"Nay[86]," said Petruchio, "I will win the wager better yet, and show more signs of her new-built virtue and obedience."

Katharine now entering with the two ladies, he continued, "See where she comes, and brings your froward[87] wives as prisoners to her womanly persuasion. Katharine, that cap of yours does not become you; off with that bauble[88], and throw it under foot."

Katharine instantly took off her cap, and threw it down.

"Lord!" said Hortensio's wife, "may I never have a cause to sigh till I am brought to such a silly pass!"

And Bianca, she too said, "Fie[89], what foolish duty call you this?"

---

86 nay [neɪ] (adv.) 〔舊時用法〕不僅如此
87 froward [ˈfrouwərd] (a.) 剛愎的；難駕馭的
88 bauble [ˈbɔːbəl] (n.) 美觀而無價值之事物
89 fie [faɪ] (int.) 〔詼諧用法〕呸

SEE WHERE SHE COMES

ACT·V·SC·II·

On this Bianca's husband said to her, "I wish your duty were as foolish too! The wisdom of your duty, fair Bianca, has cost me a hundred crowns since dinner-time."

"The more fool you," said Bianca, "for laying on my duty."

"Katharine," said Petruchio, "I charge you tell these headstrong women what duty they owe their lords and husbands."

And to the wonder of all present, the reformed shrewish lady spoke as eloquently in praise of the wifelike duty of obedience, as she had practised it implicitly[90] in a ready submission[91] to Petruchio's will.

And Katharine once more became famous in Padua, not as heretofore[92], as Katharine the Shrew, but as Katharine the most obedient and duteous wife in Padua.

---

90 implicitly [ɪmˈplɪsɪtli] (adv.)〔正式用法〕暗示地;含蓄地
91 submission [səbˈmɪʃən] (n.) 服從
92 heretofore [ˌhɪrtuˈfɔːr] (adv.) 以前;直到此時

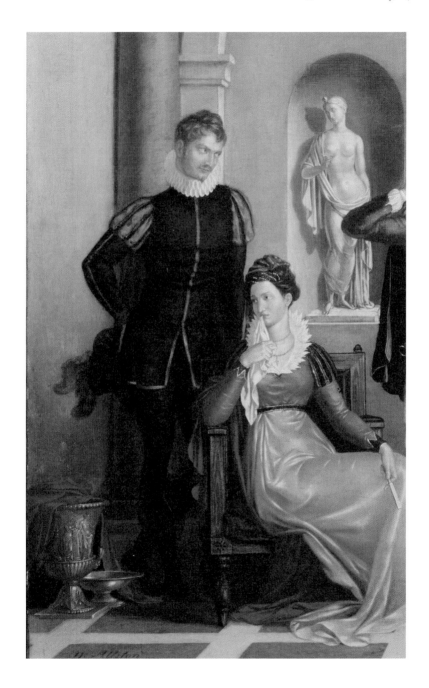

《馴悍記》名句選

Sly   Third, or fourth, or fifth borough, I'll answer him
       by law. I'll not budge an inch, boy; let him come
       and kindly. [Falls asleep]
       (Induction, i, 12–14)

斯賴   管他第三、第四、第五個官差,我沒有
       犯法。我一寸也不移,讓他來吧
       好好來。〔睡著〕
       (楔子,第一景,12-14行)

Sly   Well, we'll see. Come, madam wife, sit by my side,
       and let the world slip, we shall ne'er be younger.
       (Induction, ii, 143–144)

斯賴   好,讓我們瞧瞧。來,夫人太太,坐在我旁邊,
       我們的青春有限,管他世事滄桑。
       (楔子,第二景,143-144行)

All's Well That Ends Well

終成眷屬

《終成眷屬》導讀

女性拯救者

在民間故事裡，常可見出身低微卻擁有無比勇氣、智慧或能力的青年，在圓滿完成如屠龍、解謎、治病等最艱難的任務後，國王或公爵就會把美麗的公主許配給他。《終成眷屬》的內容與此類似，只是智勇雙全的主角變成了女性，最終的獎賞則變成了男性。

這種性別替換並非是莎士比亞自創的想法，而是源自於潘特（William Painter）於 1566–67 年間出版（1575 年修訂）的英譯故事集《愉悅的殿堂》（*The Palace of Pleasure*）。此書收錄了薄伽丘（Boccaccio）《十日談》（*Decameron*）裡第三天的第九個故事，描述女主人翁治癒國王，並兩度贏得夫婿而終成眷屬的故事。

在本劇裡，女主角海倫娜以神奇藥方治好國王的痼疾，從而得以與暗戀已久的心上人貝特漢成婚。但貝特漢不滿這椿婚姻，忿而離開家園，遠赴義大利從軍，並在當地愛上一位名為黛安娜的女子。

遭到遺棄的海倫娜傷心出走，她途經義大利時，得知丈夫的消息，便心生一計，在貝特漢即將返回法國的前一晚，假扮成黛安娜，與貝特漢共度一宵，並交換戒指作為定情物。海倫娜取得貝特漢手中的戒指後，貝特漢只得履行自己的承諾，永遠愛著海倫娜。海倫娜二度智取貝特漢，如願成為伯爵夫人，而國王也賜給黛安娜一名貴族丈夫。

此劇其實已不屬於喜劇範疇，因為在喜劇中，主要人物幾乎都要經過一番磨難後，才能獲得圓滿的結局。反觀《終成眷屬》，海倫娜歷經的各種悲喜起伏，都不像喜劇一般確定，常常與讀者的預期產生落差。例如，國王病入膏肓，御醫束手無策，而毫無經驗的海倫娜卻能憑著一帖神奇藥方讓國王康復。又例如，當貝特漢奉命與海倫娜成親，看似已經成功的計畫，卻又因貝特漢的頑固高傲讓海倫娜失望。

在一切彷彿陷入絕境之時，海倫娜竟然又巧獲貝特漢的消息，並利用一個難以令人信服的「床上把戲」（bed trick），完成另一項不可能的任務。最後，當海倫娜終於讓丈夫回頭後，國王也在此時答應讓黛安娜在群臣中挑選丈夫。

「陰鬱喜劇」和「問題劇」

整個故事看似圓滿地以喜劇收場，但讀者的預期經過三番兩次的落差後，卻不相信這是真正的結局，反而會猜想黛安娜自己挑選的婚姻，將可能會步上海倫娜與貝特漢的後塵，同樣的故事將重新上演。也因此，學者及評論家普遍認為《終成眷屬》並非喜劇，而是「陰鬱喜劇」（dark comedy）或「問題劇」（problem play）。

最早提出這個概念的是寶斯（F. S. Boas），他在 1896 年將此劇視為「問題劇」，戲中營造的「不是全然的歡愉也非全然的痛苦，但觀眾為之振奮、著迷、困惑」，而劇中的問題到最後也獲得令人滿意的結果。或許這只是指表面上令人滿意的結果，之後將引發的危機或變數，隨著劇作家停筆就嘎然而止了。

本劇沒有公開演出的紀錄，劇本在當時也沒有印行，一直到莎翁過世後七年出版的第一對開本（the First Folio）裡才出現，因此對此劇寫作年代的考證與爭論。許多人都將《終成眷屬》與《一報還一報》（*Measure for Measure*）相提並論，因為這兩齣戲都是寶斯眼中的問題劇，而且由《終成眷屬》的風格及語言特徵來推斷，此劇約完成於 1602–3 年，正好就在《一報還一報》（1604 年）之前。

本劇的韻文濃縮、簡略、抽象、模糊，也與《一報還一報》的語法相近，更有甚者，兩劇在終了時都是利用「床上把戲」，達到童話故事般的和諧結局，卻在現實世界裡顯得格格不入。

持反對意見的人則認為，類似的劇情在莎劇中出現，並不能證明寫作年代相近，例如「船難」事件就在他早期的《連環錯》（*The Comedy of Errors*）、中期的《第十二夜》（*Twelfth Night*）、晚期的《暴風雨》（*The Tempest*）裡都出現過；而《終成眷屬》的靈魂人物海倫娜為兼具膽識、智慧和美貌的女性，又與《威尼斯商人》（*The Merchant of Venice*）的波兒榭（Portia）、《皆大歡喜》（*As You Like It*）的羅莎琳（Rosalind）、《第十二夜》的菲兒拉（Viola）很像，而這些劇本都是在 1596 至 1600 年間寫成的。

儘管如此，多數學者仍將《終成眷屬》列為十七世紀的作品。因為莎翁在十七世紀初時，將主要的心思放在創作悲劇上，《哈姆雷特》（*Hamlet*）、《奧賽羅》（*Othello*）、《李爾王》（*King Lear*）、《馬克白》（*Macbeth*）都是這個階段的作品，而問題劇的主旨、調性及語言都較為接近悲劇，而不似 1590 年代後期的喜劇。

父母與女性的角色

從羅馬時期的希臘喜劇作家米南德（Menander）開始（約西元前四世紀），年輕男女會為了愛情竭盡全力跨越階級和門第之見，而老一輩的父母伯叔則是千篇一律地站在反對的另一邊。

莎翁早期的作品如《仲夏夜之夢》（*A Midsummer Night's Dream*）及《羅密歐與茱麗葉》（*Romeo and Juliet*）也遵循著這種模式，但到了《終成眷屬》，似乎是想打破這個不成文的安排，使劇中的長者展現慈愛與包容之心：國王不嫌棄海倫娜的出身，將貝特漢許配給她；老臣拉福支持她；伯爵夫人則滿心歡喜地接受她為媳婦。反之，年輕一輩的貝特漢卻顯得自視過高。

本劇的另一個特點是性別觀，其和傳統的性別角色限定有所不同。最明顯的例子是海倫娜猛追自己心儀的男子。此外，在民間故事裡，男選女之後，女方的意願無人聞問，而在這個女選男故事裡，男方的意願卻顯得很重要。

十七世紀初的監護權和對於性操守的法律規範，在英國仍受爭議。反對者認為，監護人常不考慮受監護人的個人意願，便妄自決定。贊成的人則表示，監護人有必要幫助受監護人免於外來的引誘，以免喪失地位、財產或繼承權。

監護權和性操守這兩項議題一經結合，就產生了另一項議題：「性行為究竟是屬於個人事件，還是公眾事件？」以《終成眷屬》為例，莎士比亞似乎贊成由年長者或法律條文來匡正年輕人的性觀念和性行為，引其走上婚姻的正途，例如伯爵夫人、拉福和國王都代表這一角色。

莎士比亞撰寫本劇時，他的兩個女兒都已經到了適婚年齡，因此家庭成員對於婚姻的影響力，在他的劇作裡也就愈形彰顯。從這個角度來看，本劇還標誌著莎士比亞將人物重心逐漸轉移到年長世代的過渡期。

這種轉移也獲得蕭伯納（George Bernard Shaw）的讚許，他認為，伯爵夫人是西方戲劇史上描寫得最完美的婦人，而海倫娜與貝特漢之間的情緒反應也很逼真。無怪乎若干學者不將海倫娜克服萬難的英雌事蹟視為《終成眷屬》的主旨，而是把愛情與婚姻當作此劇的核心。

《終成眷屬》人物表

Bertram	貝特漢	盧西昂伯爵,恃才傲物
Helena	海倫娜	名醫之女,愛慕貝特漢
the countess	伯爵夫人	貝特漢之母
King of France	法王	為海倫娜賜婚,許配給貝特漢
Lafeu	拉福	法國宮廷的老臣
the widow	寡婦	一個殷勤好客的寡婦
Diana	黛安娜	寡婦之女,貝特漢為她著迷

All's Well That Ends Well

Bertram, Count of Rousillon, had newly come to that title and estate, by the death of his father. The King of France loved the father of Bertram, and when he heard of his death, he sent for his son to come immediately to his royal court in Paris, intending, for the friendship he bore the late count, to grace young Bertram with his especial favour and protection.

Bertram was living with his mother, the widowed countess, when Lafeu, an old lord of the French court; came to conduct him to the king. The King of France was an absolute monarch[1] and the invitation to court was in the form of a royal mandate[2], or positive command, which no subject, of what high dignity soever, might disobey; therefore though the countess, in parting with this dear son, seemed a second time to bury her husband, whose loss she had so lately mourned, yet she dared not to keep him a single day, but gave instant orders for his departure.

Lafeu, who came to fetch him, tried to comfort the countess for the loss of her late lord, and her son's sudden absence; and he said, in a courtier's[3] flattering manner, that the king was so kind a prince, she would find in his majesty a husband, and that he would be a father to her son; meaning only, that the good king would befriend the fortunes of Bertram.

Lafeu told the countess that the king had fallen into a sad malady[4], which was pronounced by his physicians to be incurable. The lady expressed great sorrow on hearing this account of the king's ill health, and said, she wished the father of Helena (a young gentlewoman who was present in attendance upon her) were living, for that she doubted not he could have cured his majesty of his disease.

1 monarch ['mɑːnərk] (n.) 君主（國王、女王、皇帝、女皇）
2 mandate ['mændeɪt] (n.) 命令；訓令
3 courtier ['kɔːrtɪr] (n.) 朝臣（朝廷中的侍臣）
4 malady ['mælədi] (n.) 疾病

And she told Lafeu something of the history of Helena, saying she was the only daughter of the famous physician Gerard de Narbon, and that he had recommended his daughter to her care when he was dying, so that since his death she had taken Helena under her protection; then the countess praised the virtuous disposition[5] and excellent qualities of Helena, saying she inherited these virtues from her worthy father.

While she was speaking, Helena wept in sad and mournful silence, which made the countess gently reprove[6] her for too much grieving for her father's death.

Bertram now bade his mother farewell. The countess parted with this dear son with tears and many blessings, and commended[7] him to the care of Lafeu, saying, "Good my lord, advise him, for he is an unseasoned[8] courtier."

Bertram's last words were spoken to Helena, but they were words of mere civility, wishing her happiness; and he concluded his short farewell to her with saying, "Be comfortable to my mother, your mistress, and make much of her."

5　disposition [ˌdɪspəˈzɪʃən] (n.) 性情；氣質
6　reprove [rɪˈpruːv] (v.) 責備；譴責
7　commend [kəˈmend] (v.) 將……託付給……
8　unseasoned [ʌnˈsiːzənd] (a.) 無經驗的；未熟透的

Helena had long loved Bertram, and when she wept in sad and mournful silence, the tears she shed were not for Gerard de Narbon. Helena loved her father, but in the present feeling of a deeper love, the object of which she was about to lose, she had forgotten the very form and features of her dead father, her imagination presenting no image to her mind but Bertram's.

Helena had long loved Bertram, yet she always remembered that he was the Count of Rousillon, descended[9] from the most ancient family in France; she was of humble birth; her parents were of no note at all; his ancestors all noble. And therefore she looked up to the high-born Bertram as to her master and to her dear lord, and dared not form any wish but to live his servant, and so living to die his vassal[10].

So great the distance seemed to her between his height of dignity and her lowly fortunes, that she would say, "It were all one that I should love a bright particular star, and think to wed it, Bertram is so far above me."

---

9 descend [dɪ'sɛnd] (v.) （指財產、氣質、權利等）遺傳；傳代
10 vassal ['væsəl] (n.) 〔喻〕謙恭的從屬者；下屬

24

Bertram's absence filled her eyes with tears and her heart with sorrow; for though she loved without hope, yet it was a pretty comfort to her to see him every hour, and Helena would sit and look upon his dark eye, his arched brow, and the curls of his fine hair, till she seemed to draw his portrait on the tablet of her heart, that heart too capable of retaining the memory of every line in the features of that loved face.

Gerard de Narbon, when he died, left her no other portion than some prescriptions[11] of rare and well-proved virtue, which by deep study and long experience in medicine he had collected as sovereign[12] and almost infallible[13] remedies.

Among the rest, there was one set down as an approved medicine for the disease under which Lafeu said the king at that time languished[14]: and when Helena heard of the king's complaint, she, who till now had been so humble and so hopeless, formed an ambitious project in her mind to go herself to Paris, and undertake the cure of the king.

---

11 prescription [prɪˈskrɪpʃən] (n.) 所規定之事物，尤指醫生開的處方；處方上的藥

12 sovereign [ˈsɑːvrən] (a.) （指權力）至高無上的

13 infallible [ɪnˈfælɪbəl] (a.) 絕對可靠的

14 languish [ˈlæŋɡwɪʃ] (v.) 衰弱；變得無生氣

But though Helena was the possessor of this choice prescription, it was unlikely, as the king as well as his physicians was of opinion that his disease was incurable, that they would give credit to a poor unlearned virgin, if she should offer to perform a cure. The firm hopes that Helena had of succeeding, if she might be permitted to make the trial, seemed more than even her father's skill warranted, though he was the most famous physician of his time; for she felt a strong faith that this good medicine was sanctified[15] by all the luckiest stars in heaven to be the legacy[16] that should advance her fortune, even to the high dignity of being Count Rousillon's wife.

Bertram had not been long gone, when the countess was informed by her steward, that he had overheard Helena talking to herself, and that he understood from some words she uttered, she was in love with Bertram, and thought of following him to Paris. The countess dismissed the steward with thanks, and desired him to tell Helena she wished to speak with her.

15 sanctify ['sæŋktɪfaɪ] (v.) 使神聖；尊崇
16 legacy ['legəsi] (n.) 遺產；遺贈物

25

What she had just heard of Helena brought the remembrance of days long past into the mind of the countess; those days probably when her love for Bertram's father first began; and she said to herself, "Even so it was with me when I was young. Love is a thorn that belongs to the rose of youth; for in the season of youth, if ever we are nature's children, these faults are ours, though then we think not they are faults."

While the countess was thus meditating on the loving errors of her own youth, Helena entered.

And she said to her, "Helena, you know I am a mother to you."

Helena replied, "You are my honourable mistress."

"You are my daughter," said the countess again: "I say I am your mother. Why do you start and look pale at my words?"

With looks of alarm and confused thoughts, fearing the countess suspected her love, Helena still replied, "Pardon me, madam, you are not my mother; the Count Rousillon cannot be my brother, nor I your daughter."

26

"Yet, Helena," said the countess, "you might be my daughter-in-law; and I am afraid that is what you mean to be, the words mother and daughter so disturb you. Helena, do you love my son?"

"Good madam, pardon me," said the affrighted Helena.

Again the countess repeated her question, "Do you love my son?"

"Do not you love him, madam?" said Helena.

The countess replied, "Give me not this evasive[17] answer, Helena. Come, come, disclose the state of your affections, for your love has to the full appeared."

Helena on her knees now owned her love, and with shame and terror implored[18] the pardon of her noble mistress; and with words expressive of the sense she had of the inequality between their fortunes, she protested Bertram did not know she loved him, comparing her humble unaspiring[19] love to a poor Indian, who adores the sun that looks upon his worshiper, but knows of him no more.

The countess asked Helena if she had not lately an intent to go to Paris. Helena owned the design she had formed in her mind, when she heard Lafeu speak of the king's illness.

"This was your motive for wishing to go to Paris," said the countess. "Was it? Speak truly."

Helena honestly answered, "My lord your son made me to think of this; else Paris, and the medicine, and the king, had from the conversation of my thoughts been absent then."

The countess heard the whole of this confession without saying a word either of approval or of blame, but she strictly questioned Helena as to the probability of the medicine being useful to the king.

17 evasive [ɪ'veɪsɪv] (a.) 躲避的；逃避的
18 implore [ɪm'plɔːr] (v.) 懇求；哀求
19 unaspiring [ˌʌnə'spaɪərɪŋ] (a.) 追求不到的

27 She found that it was the most prized by Gerard de Narbon of all he possessed, and that he had given it to his daughter on his deathbed; and remembering the solemn promise she had made at that awful hour in regard to this young maid, whose destiny and the life of the king himself, seemed to depend on the execution of a project (which though conceived[20] by the fond suggestions of a loving maiden's thoughts, the countess knew not but it might be the unseen workings of Providence[21] to bring to pass the recovery of the king, and to lay the foundation of the future fortunes of Gerard de Narbon's daughter), free leave she gave to Helena to pursue her own way, and generously furnished her with ample[22] means and suitable attendants and Helena set out for Paris with the blessings of the countess, and her kindest wishes for her success.

---

20 conceive [kən'siːv] (v.) 構思；計畫
21 Providence ['prɑːvɪdəns] (n.) 〔作大寫〕上帝；天佑
22 ample ['æmpəl] (a.) 充足的；豐富的

Helena arrived at Paris, and by the assistance of her friend the old Lord Lafeu, she obtained an audience of the king. She had still many difficulties to encounter, for the king was not easily prevailed[23] on to try the medicine offered him by this fair young doctor. But she told him she was Gerard de Narbon's daughter (with whose fame the king was well acquainted) and she offered the precious medicine as the darling treasure which contained the essence of all her father's long experience and skill, and she boldly engaged to forfeit[24] her life, if it failed to restore his majesty to perfect health in the space of two days.

23 prevail [prɪˈveɪl] (v.) 勸導
24 forfeit [ˈfɔːrfit] (v.)（因懲罰結果或規則等）喪失

King. Now, fair one, does your business follow us?
Helena. Ay, my good lord.

Act II. Scene I.

The king at length consented to try it, and in two days' time Helena was to lose her life if the king did not recover; but if she succeeded, he promised to give her the choice of any man throughout all France (the princes only excepted) whom she could like for a husband; the choice of a husband being the fee Helena demanded if she cured the king of his disease.

Helena did not deceive herself in the hope she conceived of the efficacy[25] of her father's medicine. Before two days were at an end, the king was restored to perfect health, and he assembled all the young noblemen of his court together, in order to confer[26] the promised reward of a husband upon his fair physician; and he desired Helena to look round on this youthful parcel of noble bachelors, and choose her husband.

Helena was not slow to make her choice, for among these young lords she saw the Count Rousillon, and turning to Bertram, she said, "This is the man. I dare not say, my lord I take you, but I give me and my service ever whilst[27] I live into your guiding power."

25 efficacy ['efɪkəsi] (n.) （不用於指人）有效；效能
26 confer [kənˈfɜːr] (v.) 授與（學位、頭銜、恩惠）
27 whilst [hwaɪlst] (conj.) 當⋯⋯的時候

"Why, then," said the king, "young Bertram, take her; she is your wife."

Bertram did not hesitate to declare his dislike to this present of the king's of the self-offered Helena, who, he said, was a poor physician's daughter, bred at his father's charge, and now living a dependent on his mother's bounty[28].

Helena heard him speak these words of rejection and of scorn[29], and she said to the king, "That you are well, my lord, I am glad. Let the rest go."

But the king would not suffer his royal command to be so slighted; for the power of bestowing[30] their nobles in marriage was one of the many privileges of the kings of France; and that same day Bertram was married to Helena, a forced and uneasy marriage to Bertram, and of no promising hope to the poor lady, who, though she gained the noble husband she had hazarded[31] her life to obtain, seemed to have won but a splendid blank, her husband's love not being a gift in the power of the King of France to bestow.

---

28 bounty ['baʊnti] (n.) 〔正式〕慷慨；好施
29 scorn [skɔːrn] (n.) 輕蔑；蔑視
30 bestow [bɪ'stoʊ] (v.) 給與；授與；賜贈
31 hazard ['hæzərd] (v.) 冒……之險；遭受……危險

Helena was no sooner married, than she was desired by Bertram to apply to the king for him for leave of absence from court; and when she brought him the king's permission for his departure, Bertram told her that he was not prepared for this sudden marriage, it had much unsettled him, and therefore she must not wonder at the course he should pursue.

If Helena wondered not, she grieved when she found it was his intention to leave her.

He ordered her to go home to his mother. When Helena heard this unkind command, she replied, "Sir, I can nothing say to this, but that I am your most obedient servant, and shall ever with true observance[32] seek to eke[33] out that desert, wherein my homely stars have failed to equal my great fortunes."

But this humble speech of Helena's did not at all move the haughty[34] Bertram to pity his gentle wife, and he parted from her without even the common civility of a kind farewell.

32 observance [əbˈzɜːrvəns] (n.)（法律、習俗、節日等）遵守；奉行
33 eke [iːk] (v.) 補足；力求維持（生活）
34 haughty [ˈhɔːti] (a.) 傲慢的；驕傲的

【31】 Back to the countess then Helena returned. She had accomplished the purport[35] of her journey, she had preserved the life of the king, and she had wedded her heart's dear lord, the Count Rousillon; but she returned back a dejected lady to her noble mother-in-law, and as soon as she entered the house she received a letter from Bertram which almost broke her heart.

The good countess received her with a cordial[36] welcome, as if she had been her son's own choice, and a lady of a high degree, and she spoke kind words to comfort her for the unkind neglect of Bertram in sending his wife home on her bridal day alone.

But this gracious reception failed to cheer the sad mind of Helena, and she said, "Madam, my lord is gone, forever gone."

She then read these words out of Bertram's letter:

> When you can get the ring from my finger, which never shall come off, then call me husband, but in such a Then I write a Never.

"This is a dreadful sentence!" said Helena.

The countess begged her to have patience, and said, now Bertram was gone, she should be her child, and that she deserved a lord that twenty such rude boys as Bertram might tend upon, and hourly call her mistress. But in vain by respectful condescension[37] and kind flattery this matchless mother tried to soothe[38] the sorrows of her daughter-in-law.

Helena still kept her eyes fixed upon the letter, and cried out in an agony[39] of grief,

> *Till I have no wife,*
> *I have nothing in France.*

The countess asked her if she found those words in the letter.

"Yes, madam," was all poor Helena could answer.

---

35 purport [pɜːrˈpɔːrt] (n.)〔正式〕主旨；意義；一個人的行為之可能解釋

36 cordial [ˈkɔːrdʒəl] (a.)（在情感或行為上）熱誠；懇摯的

37 condescension [ˌkɑːndɪˈsenʃən] (n.) 屈尊；俯就

38 soothe [suːð] (v.)（使痛苦或疼痛）緩和或減輕

39 agony [ˈæɡəni] (n.)（精神或肉體上的）極大的痛苦

🎧 32 The next morning Helena was missing. She left a letter to be delivered to the countess after she was gone, to acquaint her with the reason of her sudden absence: in this letter she informed her that she was so much grieved at having driven Bertram from his native country and his home, that to atone[40] for her offense, she had undertaken a pilgrimage[41] to the shrine of St. Jaques le Grand, and concluded with requesting the countess to inform her son that the wife he so hated had left his house forever.

Bertram, when he left Paris, went to Florence, and there became an officer in the Duke of Florence's army, and after a successful war, in which he distinguished himself by many brave actions, Bertram received letters from his mother, containing the acceptable tidings[42] that Helena would no more disturb him.

And he was preparing to return home, when Helena herself, clad[43] in her pilgrim's weeds, arrived at the city of Florence.

---

40 atone [əˈtoʊn] (v.) 彌補;補償;贖罪
41 pilgrimage [ˈpɪlɡrɪmɪdʒ] (n.) 朝聖者的旅程
42 tidings [ˈtaɪdɪŋz] (n.) 〔古〕消息;音信
43 clad [klæd] (v.) 使披上（clothe 的舊式過去分詞）

Florence was a city through which the pilgrims used to pass on their way to St. Jaques le Grand; and when Helena arrived at this city, she heard that a hospitable widow dwelt there, who used to receive into her house the female pilgrims that were going to visit the shrine of that saint, giving them lodging and kind entertainment. To this good lady, therefore, Helena went, and the widow gave her a courteous welcome, and invited her to see whatever was curious in that famous city, and told her that if she would like to see the duke's army, she would take her where she might have a full view of it.

"And you will see a countryman of yours," said the widow; "his name is Count Rousillon, who has done worthy service in the duke's wars."

Helena wanted no second invitation, when she found Bertram was to make part of the show. She accompanied her hostess; and a sad and mournful pleasure it was to her to look once more upon her dear husband's face.

Is he not a handsome man?" said the widow.

"I like him well," replied Helena, with great truth.

All the way they walked, the talkative widow's discourse was all of Bertram: she told Helena the story of Bertram's marriage, and how he had deserted the poor lady his wife, and entered into the duke's army to avoid living with her.

To this account of her own misfortunes Helena patiently listened, and when it was ended, the history of Bertram was not yet done, for then the widow began another tale, every word of which sank deep into the mind of Helena; for the story she now told was of Bertram's love for her daughter.

Though Bertram did not like the marriage forced on him by the king, it seems he was not insensible to love, for since he had been stationed[44] with the army at Florence, he had fallen in love with Diana, a fair young gentlewoman, the daughter of this widow who was Helena's hostess; and every night, with music of all sorts, and songs composed in praise of Diana's beauty, he would come under her window, and solicit[45] her love; and all his suit to her was, that she would permit him to visit her by stealth after the family were retired to rest.

44 station [ˈsteɪʃən] (v.) 安置；配置
45 solicit [səˈlɪsɪt] (v.) 懇求；乞求

35

But Diana would by no means be persuaded to grant this improper request, nor give any encouragement to his suit, knowing him to be a married man; for Diana had been brought up under the counsels[46] of a prudent mother, who, though she was now in reduced circumstances, was well born, and descended from the noble family of the Capulets.

All this the good lady related to Helena, highly praising the virtuous principles of her discreet daughter, which she said were entirely owing to the excellent education and good advice she had given her; and she further said, that Bertram had been particularly importunate[47] with Diana to admit him to the visit he so much desired that night, because he was going to leave Florence early the next morning.

Though it grieved Helena to hear of Bertram's love for the widow's daughter, yet from this story the ardent[48] mind of Helena conceived a project (nothing discouraged at the ill success of her former one) to recover her truant[49] lord.

She disclosed to the widow that she was Helena, the deserted wife of Bertram and requested that her kind hostess and her daughter would suffer this visit from Bertram to take place, and allow her to pass herself upon Bertram for Diana; telling them, her chief motive for desiring to have this secret meeting with her husband, was to get a ring from him, which he had said, if ever she was in possession of he would acknowledge her as his wife.

The widow and her daughter promised to assist her in this affair, partly moved by pity for this unhappy forsaken wife, and partly won over to her interest by the promises of reward which Helena made them, giving them a purse of money in earnest of her future favour.

In the course of that day Helena caused information to be sent to Bertram that she was dead; hoping that when he thought himself free to make a second choice by the news of her death, he would offer marriage to her in her feigned[50] character of Diana. And if she could obtain the ring and this promise too, she doubted not she should make some future good come of it.

---

46 counsel ['kaʊnsəl] (n.) 勸告；忠告
47 importunate [ɪmˈpɔːrtʃʊnɪt] (a.)（指事務等）急切的
48 ardent ['ɑːrdənt] (a.) 熱心的；熱情的
49 truant ['truːənt] (a.)（思想、行為等）怠惰的；規避（責任）的
50 feigned [feɪnd] (a.) 假裝的

36

In the evening, after it was dark, Bertram was admitted into Diana's chamber, and Helena was there ready to receive him.

The flattering compliments and love discourse he addressed to Helena were precious sounds to her, though she knew they were meant for Diana; and Bertram was so well pleased with her, that he made her a solemn promise to be her husband, and to love her forever; which she hoped would be prophetic of a real affection, when he should know it was his own wife, the despised Helena, whose conversation had so delighted him.

Bertram never knew how sensible a lady Helena was, else perhaps he would not have been so regardless of her; and seeing her every day, he had entirely overlooked her beauty; a face we are accustomed to see constantly, losing the effect which is caused by the first sight either of beauty or of plainness; and of her understanding it was impossible he should judge, because she felt such reverence, mixed with her love for him, that she was always silent in his presence.

[37] But now that her future fate, and the happy ending of all her love-projects, seemed to depend on her leaving a favourable impression on the mind of Bertram from this night's interview, she exerted[51] all her wit to please him; and the simple graces of her lively conversation and the endearing sweetness of her manners so charmed Bertram, that he vowed she should be his wife.

Helena begged the ring from off his finger as a token[52] of his regard, and he gave it to her; and in return for this ring, which it was of such importance to her to possess, she gave him another ring, which was one the king had made her a present of.

Before it was light in the morning, she sent Bertram away; and he immediately set out on his journey toward his mother's house.

Helena prevailed on the widow and Diana to accompany her to Paris, their further assistance being necessary to the full accomplishment of the plan she had formed. When they arrived there, they found the king was gone upon a visit to the Countess of Rousillon, and Helena followed the king with all the speed she could make.

The king was still in perfect health, and his gratitude to her who had been the means of his recovery was so lively in his mind, that the moment he saw the Countess of Rousillon, he began to talk of Helena, calling her a precious jewel that was lost by the folly of her son; but seeing the subject distressed the countess, who sincerely lamented[53] the death of Helena, he said, "My good lady, I have forgiven and forgotten all."

But the good-natured old Lafeu, who was present, and could not bear that the memory of his favourite Helena should be so lightly passed over, said, "This I must say, the young lord did great offense to his majesty, his mother, and his lady; but to himself he did the greatest wrong of all, for he has lost a wife whose beauty astonished all eyes, whose words took all ears captive[54], whose deep perfection made all hearts wish to serve her."

51　exert [ɪgˈzɜːrt] (v.) 發揮；運用
52　token [ˈtoʊkən] (n.) 證據；象徵；記號
53　lament [ləˈment] (v.) 悲傷；惋惜
54　captive [ˈkæptɪv] (a.) 被俘的；被迷住的
　　(n.) 俘虜；被俘虜的（人）；被捕獲的（動物）

The king said, "Praising what is lost makes the remembrance dear. Well—call him hither;" meaning Bertram, who now presented himself before the king: and on his expressing deep sorrow for the injuries he had done to Helena, the king, for his dead father's and his admirable mother's sake, pardoned him and restored him once more to his favour.

But the gracious countenance of the king was soon changed toward him, for he perceived that Bertram wore the very ring upon his finger which he had given to Helena: and he well remembered that Helena had called all the saints in heaven to witness she would never part with that ring, unless she sent it to the king himself upon some great disaster befalling her; and Bertram, on the king's questioning him how he came by the ring, told an improbable story of a lady throwing it to him out of a window, and denied ever having seen Helena since the day of their marriage.

The king, knowing Bertram's dislike to his wife, feared he had destroyed her: and he ordered his guards to seize Bertram, saying, "I am wrapt in dismal[55] thinking, for I fear the life of Helena was foully snatched."

---

55 dismal ['dɪzməl] (a.) 憂愁的

At this moment Diana and her mother entered, and presented a petition[56] to the king, wherein they begged his majesty to exert his royal power to compel[57] Bertram to marry Diana, he having made her a solemn promise of marriage. Bertram, fearing the king's anger, denied he had made any such promise; and then Diana produced the ring (which Helena had put into her hands) to confirm the truth of her words; and she said that she had given Bertram the ring he then wore, in exchange for that, at the time he vowed to marry her.

On hearing this the king ordered the guards to seize her also; and her account of the ring differing from Bertram's, the king's suspicions were confirmed: and he said, if they did not confess how they came by this ring of Helena's, they should be both put to death.

Diana requested her mother might be permitted to fetch the jeweller of whom she bought the ring, which being granted, the widow went out, and presently returned, leading in Helena herself.

The good countess, who in silent grief had beheld her son's danger, and had even dreaded that the suspicion of his having destroyed his wife might possibly be

true, finding her dear Helena, whom she loved with even a maternal[58] affection, was still living, felt a delight she was hardly able to support; and the king, scarce believing for joy that it was Helena, said, "Is this indeed the wife of Bertram that I see?"

56 petition [pɪ'tɪʃən] (n.) 請願書；陳情書
57 compel [kəm'pel] (v.) 強迫；迫使
58 maternal [mə'tɜːrnl] (a.) 母親的；似母親的

 Helena, feeling herself yet an unacknowledged wife, replied, "No, my good lord, it is but the shadow of a wife you see, the name and not the thing."

Bertram cried out, "Both, both! Oh pardon!"

"O my lord," said Helena, "when I personated[59] this fair maid, I found you wondrous kind; and look, here is your letter!" reading to him in a joyful tone those words which she had once repeated so sorrowfully, "When from my finger you can get this ring—This is done; it was to me you gave the ring. Will you be mine, now you are doubly won?"

Bertram replied, "If you can make it plain that you were the lady I talked with that night, I will love you dearly ever, ever dearly."

This was no difficult task, for the widow and Diana came with Helena to prove this fact; and the king was so well pleased with Diana for the friendly assistance she had rendered[60] the dear lady he so truly valued for the service she had done him, that he promised her also a noble husband: Helena's history giving him a hint, that it was a suitable reward for kings to bestow upon fair ladies when they perform notable services.

Thus Helena at last found that her father's legacy was indeed sanctified by the luckiest stars in heaven; for she was now the beloved wife of her dear Bertram, the daughter-in-law of her noble mistress, and herself the Countess of Rousillon.

---

59 personate ['pɜːrsəneɪt] (v.) 扮演；飾演（戲中某一角色）
60 render ['rendər] (v.) 呈遞；提供

《終成眷屬》名句選

Lafeu   I have seen a medicine
That's able to breathe life into a stone,
Quicken a rock, and make you dance canary
With spritely fire and motion, whose simple
    touch
Is powerful to araise King Pippen, nay
To give great Charlemain a pen in's hand
And write to her a love-line.
(II, i, 72–78)

拉福   我剛看到一種藥,
能讓石子活起來,
能賦與岩塊生命,能使您翩然起舞
能讓您生龍活虎;它可以輕輕鬆鬆
讓培平大王復活,不只如此
還可以教查理曼大帝執起筆來,
為她寫下一行情詩。
(第二幕,第一景,72–78行)

Countess If ever we are nature's, these are ours; this thorn
Doth to our rose of youth rightly belong;
Our blood to us, this to our blood is born;
It is the show and seal of nature's truth,
Where love's strong passion is impress'd in youth:
By our remembrances of days foregone,
Such were our faults, or then we thought them none.
(I, iii, 41–47)

伯爵夫人 我們是自然之子，擁有自然的感情；
這一根刺，是青春的薔薇上少不了的。
有了我們，就有感情；有了感情，就少不了這根刺。
當熱烈的愛戀烙印在青春裡，
這是自然天性的流露與痕跡。
在我們往日的回憶裡，我們會犯這樣的錯，
而我們當時並不認為那有什麼不對。

（第一幕，第三景，41–47 行）

Measure for Measure

一報還一報

《一報還一報》導讀

故事來源

在十六世紀的歐洲，美貌女子被迫獻身以保全親人的性命是很常見的故事。《一報還一報》主要的故事來源是英國劇作家匯斯東（George Whetstone）於 1578 年所寫的《波莫思與卡珊卓》（*Promos and Cassandra*）。這個不受歡迎也不曾演出的劇本，靈感得自於義大利的辛提歐（Giraldi Cinthio）所撰寫的《百則故事》（*Gli Hecatommithi*）。這兩位作者分別將這個故事寫了小說與戲劇兩種版本。莎翁根據這兩個版本創造瑪莉安娜一角，並決定讓公爵偽裝成修士，之後睹整個事件的過程。

演出記錄

據記載，1604 年本劇曾在英國國王詹姆士一世御前演出，當時為全新的劇作。1603 年五月至隔年四月，倫敦的劇院因瘟疫被迫關閉，所以一般推測此劇完成的年代是 1604 年。

這齣戲雖然在第一版的莎翁全集第一對開本（the First Folio）裡被列為喜劇，但是直到最後「喜劇」收場為止，劇情的發展都缺乏喜劇感。

當此時期，是莎翁創作悲劇的登峰時期：他在 1603–4 年創作了《奧塞羅》，1604–5 年完成《李爾王》，1606 年又推出《馬克白》。故依常理判斷，他應該不會在這段期間寫出如此受爭議的劇本，因此有部分學者認為，可能是莎翁自己在此時遭逢了人生的巨大創痛。

歷史紀錄顯示，本劇首演之後，經過了一甲子，才有機會重新搬演。而且這齣戲自十八世紀開始，一直到二十世紀為止，在舞台上的評價都不甚優良，劇本也鮮少獲得批評家的讚賞。

席德尼爵士（Sir Philip Sidney）說：「喜劇就是模仿生活中的誤會，用滑稽可笑的方式呈現，使觀眾認為絕對不可能發生。」從這兩個角度來看，稱《一報還一報》為喜劇並不為過。莎士比亞似乎在他早期的劇場生涯就已經認為：歷經一連串的道德衝突或生命危險之後，達到圓滿結局，才算是喜劇收場。

負面評價

主要的原因是情節不合常理，結局又顯得突兀。1754 年，藍納（Charlotte Lennox）曾將此劇和辛提歐的原作互相比較，並撰文表示莎翁的改編愈改愈差，劇中只見「低等的計畫、荒謬的情節、不合情理的事件……為的就是讓一群人結婚，也不願以斬首作收。」

發表過眾多精闢莎劇見解的十九世紀文人兼批評家柯立芝（Coleridge），則稱此劇為「討厭的戲」，是莎翁「唯一令人痛苦的戲」。劇中的喜劇情節讓人生厭，悲劇情節讓人害怕：安哲羅可以說是犯了謀殺與強暴未遂兩項罪行，但劇終的正義

卻完全只由寬恕取代；伊莎貝拉也不怎麼討人喜歡，她重視貞操的程度遠勝於親兄弟的性命；伊莎貝拉的弟弟則是個懦弱青年，自己犯錯卻期望姐姐犧牲貞操來換取自己的性命。

故事主題

劇中涉及諸多概念，包括道德、性欲、死亡、公權力的運用與濫用，以及人在關鍵時期所流露的本性和情感。本劇的劇名出自《新約聖經 ·馬太福音》第七章：「不要審判，免得你們受審判。你們用什麼審判審判人，也必受什麼審判；你們用什麼量器量別人，也必用什麼量器被量。」如劇中，安哲羅即使魔高一尺，也終究要由道高一丈的公爵，以其人之道還治其人之身。

安哲羅雖然享有無瑕盛名，但當伊莎貝拉為被判死刑的弟弟求情時，他竟向伊莎貝拉提出以貞節作為換取條件，暴露他雙重的違法傾向——知法犯法（無夫妻之實而發生性行為者，依法必須處死），以及瀆職（因個人因素而未執行法律，使克勞狄免於一死）。然而一夜溫存之後，他又殘暴地下令將克勞狄處死，因而犯下了道義上的誆騙之罪和未婚性交的死罪。

但這一切並不能證明他就是個不折不扣的偽君子，他為自己的色欲備受煎熬，一方面憎惡自己醜陋的罪行，另一方面又強烈受到純潔的伊莎貝拉所吸引，最後還受到一股莫名的力量驅使他殺害克勞狄，以掩飾自己的貪欲。事發之後，他也不求寬容，只想以死抵罪。但他就像《終成眷屬》的貝特漢及《無事生非》的克勞迪一樣，都犯下大錯，卻在劇終時獲得寬恕。

伊莎貝拉和安哲羅雖然處於對立的立場，卻有巧合的雷同之處：崇尚精神與修行，過著與世隔絕的生活。安哲羅的行為與聲譽背道而馳，伊莎貝拉表裡如一，但她一樣無法獲得眾人的掌聲。一般人之所以對她不表示全然贊同，並不是因為她提倡慈悲或是矜持守節，而是因為性命不保的弟弟乞求她時，她仍給予無情的教訓。

伊莎貝拉在聖克萊兒修道院時，就希望院方能有更嚴謹的清規，事實上那已是羅馬天主教中最嚴格的教堂了。安哲羅要求她以身相報時，她被迫在「凜然赴死」與「含辱救弟」之間做一抉擇，她毫不考慮就選擇前者，並義正辭嚴教訓弟弟，甚至懷著仇恨似地要臨死的弟弟也應抱持相同的看法。

她和安哲羅一樣，對人性只有善惡對立的二分法。她請求公爵饒恕安哲羅，展現了高尚情操，但或許她並非懇求公爵原諒她的敵人，而是請求他饒瑪莉安娜的未婚夫一命。

偽裝成修士的公爵，目睹純潔、沉淪和絕望的全部過程，然後在悲劇即將一發不可收拾之時，及時介入，挽救伊莎貝拉的貞節和克勞狄的性命。他還試驗他所觀察的人，如安哲羅、伊莎貝拉等，儼然像是無所不在的上帝。

公爵一角具有許多爭議：愛民卻愛得不得其法，使得維也納城道德敗壞；怠忽職守卻不加以改進，反而決定由代理人安哲羅代為導正，以逃避自己執法時可能遭致的批評及抗拒；他企圖操控所有的角色，懷疑安哲羅只是「看似聖人」，似乎早料到他會出錯；克勞狄即將處死，充滿恐懼，他卻只能提供基督教的思想教誨，勸誠他平和安詳地告別這個世界；更令人不可置信的是，公爵竟然以「床上把戲」（bed trick）當作解決方法，要瑪莉安娜代替伊莎貝拉與安哲羅共度一夜，等於又犯下克勞狄與茱麗葉犯過的罪。因此，雖然他在劇終時彷彿是從天而降的正義之神，對相關的人施予懲罰及寬恕，但是因為代理事件而引發的種種痛苦、羞辱、憤怒與恐懼，他其實應該要負最大的責任。

大臣艾斯卡是本劇裡頭的折衷角色，他不像伊莎貝拉和安哲羅，對道德抱持極端嚴厲的態度，也不像公爵採取完全放任的立場。他的所作所為合情合理，以現實的眼光衡量事件的嚴重程度與處理方式，並以耐心和毅力解決政務問題。他贊成公爵的改革，又為克勞狄所處的境況求情。雖然如此，他沒有相對的權力執法，也無法使惡行因此而減少。法律規範期望的是能

Mariana

以外在的懲處，淨化內在的想法，而不應該一味要求人人都成
為聖人，或永無止境地原諒罪人。

重新定位

時至二十世紀初，開始有批評家認為不應再以十九世紀自然
主義的閱讀習慣來看待《一報還一報》，而應將其視為以戲劇
面貌呈現的寓言故事，用以宣揚基督教高貴的精神。少數不
贊同上述說法的學者，紛紛將此劇歸類為「悲喜劇」（tragi-
comedy），認為劇中的宗教意義、戲劇表現、人物塑造等等，
都接近莎翁的戲劇風格及當時的民俗故事，而非單純的宣揚教
義之作。

莎翁時期的人也可能將《一報還一報》視為悲喜劇。義大利劇
作家郭里尼（Giambattista Guarini）曾在 1601 年出版的著作
《悲喜詩學概述》（*Compendium of Tragi-Comic Poetry*）中提
到：悲喜劇是分別由悲劇與喜劇中擷取適當的成分，組合而成
的第三種戲劇類型，具有悲劇的情節及險境，卻不包括悲劇的
痛楚與死亡，同時又含有喜劇中的歡笑、娛樂、喜劇式逆轉和
愉快結局。由開場時克勞狄的處境、伊莎貝拉的懇求或安哲羅
的鐵石心腸來檢視本劇，將其歸為悲喜劇似乎並無不妥。

此外，當代也有評論家將此劇與《終成眷屬》一起視為「問題
劇」（problem play）或「陰鬱喜劇」（dark comedy）。最早
提出這個概念的是寶斯（F. S. Boas），他在 1896 年將此劇視為
問題劇，並加以解釋：戲中營造的「不是全然的歡愉也非全然
的痛苦，但我們卻為之振奮、著迷、困惑」，而劇中的問題，
到最後也獲得令人滿意的結果。

《一報還一報》人物表

the duke	公爵	維也納一位公爵，之後假扮成修士
Angelo	安哲羅	公爵的代理者
Claudio	克勞狄	因為被控誘拐女子而被關進監牢
Escalus	艾斯卡	公爵的一位老臣
Lucio	陸西歐	克勞狄的友人
Isabel	伊莎貝拉	克勞狄的姊姊
Juliet	茱麗葉	克勞狄被控誘拐的女孩
Mariana	瑪莉安娜	安哲羅的未婚妻

Measure for Measure

〔41〕 In the city of Vienna there once reigned a duke of such a mild and gentle temper, that he suffered his subjects to neglect the laws with impunity[1]; and there was in particular one law, the existence of which was almost forgotten, the duke never having put it in force during his whole reign.

This was a law dooming any man to the punishment of death, who should live with a woman that was not his wife; and this law, through the lenity[2] of the duke, being utterly disregarded, the holy institution of marriage became neglected, and complaints were every day made to the duke by the parents of the young ladies in Vienna, that their daughters had been seduced[3] from their protection, and were living as the companions of single men.

---

1 impunity [ɪmˈpjuːnɪti] (n.) 免受懲罰
2 lenity [ˈlenəti] (n.) 〔正式〕慈悲；寬厚
3 seduce [sɪˈdjuːs] (v.) 勾引；誘姦

The good duke perceived with sorrow this growing evil among his subjects; but he thought that a sudden change in himself from the indulgence he had hitherto shown, to the strict severity requisite[4] to check this abuse, would make his people (who had hitherto loved him) consider him as a tyrant.

Therefore he determined to absent himself a while from his dukedom, and depute[5] another to the full exercise of his power, that the law against these dishonourable lovers might be put in effect, without giving offense by an unusual severity in his own person.

Angelo, a man who bore the reputation of a saint in Vienna for his strict and rigid life, was chosen by the duke as a fit person to undertake this important charge; and when the duke imparted[6] his design to Lord Escalus, his chief counsellor, Escalus said, "If any man in Vienna be of worth to undergo such ample grace and honour, it is Lord Angelo."

4 requisite ['rekwɪzɪt] (a.) 需要的；必要的
5 depute [dɪ'pjuːt] (v.) 將（工作、職權等）交予代理人
6 impart [ɪm'pɑːrt] (v.) 〔正式〕透露；通知；告知

MEASURE
FOR
MEASURE.

And now the duke departed from Vienna under pretence of making a journey into Poland, leaving Angelo to act as the lord deputy in his absence; but the duke's absence was only a feigned one, for he privately returned to Vienna, habited like a friar[7], with the intent to watch unseen the conduct of the saintly-seeming Angelo.

It happened just about the time that Angelo was invested with his new dignity, that a gentleman, whose name was Claudio, had seduced a young lady from her parents; and for this offense, by command of the new lord deputy, Claudio was taken up and committed to prison, and by virtue of the old law which had been so long neglected, Angelo sentenced Claudio to be beheaded.

Great interest was made for the pardon of young Claudio, and the good old Lord Escalus himself interceded[8] for him. "Alas," said he, "this gentleman whom I would save had an honourable father, for whose sake I pray you pardon the young man's transgression[9]."

---

7 friar ['fraɪər] (n.) 修道士；修士
8 intercede [ˌɪntər'siːd] (v.) （為調停或為獲得贊助而）說項；求情
9 transgression [træns'greʃən] (n.) 逾越；違犯；道德犯罪

🎧 43 But Angelo replied, "We must not make a scarecrow[10] of the law, setting it up to frighten birds of prey, till custom, finding it harmless, makes it their perch[11], and not their terror. Sir, he must die."

Lucio, the friend of Claudio, visited him in the prison, and Claudio said to him, "I pray you, Lucio, do me this kind service. Go to my sister Isabel, who this day proposes to enter the convent[12] of Saint Clare; acquaint her with the danger of my state; implore her that she make friends with the strict deputy; bid her go herself to Angelo. I have great hopes in that; for she can discourse with prosperous art, and well she can persuade; besides, there is a speechless dialect in youthful sorrow, such as moves men."

Isabel, the sister of Claudio, had, as he said, that day entered upon her novitiate[13] in the convent, and it was her intent, after passing through her probation[14] as a novice[15], to take the veil, and she was inquiring of a nun concerning the rules of the convent, when they heard the voice of Lucio, who, as he entered that religious house, said, "Peace be in this place!"

"Who is it that speaks?" said Isabel.

10 scarecrow [ˈskerkroʊ] (n.) 稻草人

11 perch [pɜːrtʃ] (n.) 鳥的棲息之所（如樹枝）；棲木

12 convent [ˈkɑːnvent] (n.) 女修道會；修女會

13 novitiate [noʊˈvɪʃɪət] (n.) 做見習修士或修女；見習期

14 probation [proʊˈbeɪʃən] (n.) 見習

15 novice [ˈnɑːvɪs] (n.) 見習修士或修女

44

"It is a man's voice," replied the nun: "Gentle Isabel, go to him, and learn his business; you may, I may not. When you have taken the veil, you must not speak with men but in the presence of the prioress[16]; then if you speak you must not show your face, or if you show your face, you must not speak."

"And have you nuns no further privileges?" said Isabel.

"Are not these large enough?" replied the nun.

"Yes, truly," said Isabel: "I speak not as desiring more, but rather wishing a more strict restraint upon the sisterhood, the votarists[17] of Saint Clare."

Again they heard the voice of Lucio, and the nun said, "He calls again. I pray you answer him."

Isabel then went out to Lucio, and in answer to his salutation, said, "Peace and Prosperity! Who is it that calls?"

Then Lucio, approaching her with reverence, said, "Hail[18], virgin, if such you be, as the roses on your cheeks proclaim you are no less! can you bring me to the sight of Isabel, a novice of this place, and the fair sister to her unhappy brother Claudio?"

16 prioress [ˈpraɪərɪs] (n.) 小女修道院院長

17 votarist [ˈvoutərɪst] (n.) 熱心者；(尤指宗教工作的)支持者

18 hail [heɪl] (v.) 歡迎；向……招呼(以引其注意)

45

"Why her unhappy brother?" said Isabel, "let me ask! for I am that Isabel, and his sister."

"Fair and gentle lady," he replied, "your brother kindly greets you by me; he is in prison."

"Woe[19] is me! for what?" said Isabel.

Lucio then told her, Claudio was imprisoned for seducing a young maiden.

"Ah," said she, "I fear it is my cousin Juliet."

Juliet and Isabel were not related, but they called each other cousin in remembrance of their school days' friendship; and as Isabel knew that Juliet loved Claudio, she feared she had been led by her affection for him into this transgression.

"She it is," replied Lucio.

"Why, then, let my brother marry Juliet," said Isabel.

Lucio replied that Claudio would gladly marry Juliet, but that the lord deputy had sentenced him to die for his offense. "Unless," said he, "you have the grace by your fair prayer to soften Angelo, and that is my business between you and your poor brother."

"Alas!" said Isabel, "what poor ability is there in me to do him good? I doubt I have no power to move Angelo."

"Our doubts are traitors," said Lucio, "and make us lose the good we might often win, by fearing to attempt it. Go to Lord Angelo! When maidens sue, and kneel, and weep, men give like gods."

"I will see what I can do", said Isabel: "I will but stay to give the prioress notice of the affair, and then I will go to Angelo. Commend me to my brother: soon at night I will send him word of my success."

Isabel hastened to the palace, and threw herself on her knees before Angelo, saying, "I am a woeful suitor to your honour, if it will please your honour to hear me."

"Well, what is your suit?" said Angelo.

She then made her petition in the most moving terms for her brother's life.

19 woe [wou] (int.)（表示痛苦或悲傷）哎呀

142

But Angelo said, "Maiden, there is no remedy; your brother is sentenced, and he must die."

"Oh just, but severe law," said Isabel: "I had a brother then—heaven keep your honour!" and she was about to depart.

But Lucio, who had accompanied her, said, "Give it not over so; return to him again, entreat him, kneel down before him, hang upon his gown. You are too cold; if you should need a pin, you could not with a more tame tongue desire it."

Then again Isabel on her knees implored for mercy.

"He is sentenced," said Angelo: "It is too late."

"Too late!" said Isabel. "Why, no! I that do speak a word may call it back again. Believe this, my lord, no ceremony that to great ones belongs, not the king's crown, nor the deputed sword, the marshal's[20] truncheon[21], nor the judge's robe, becomes them with one half so good a grace as mercy does."

---

20 marshal ['mɑːrʃəl] (n.) 最高級軍官；元帥
21 truncheon ['trʌntʃən] (n.) 官杖；司令杖

"Pray you begone," said Angelo.

But still Isabel entreated; and she said, "If my brother had been as you, and you as he, you might have slipped like him, but he, like you, would not have been so stern. I would to heaven I had your power, and you were Isabel. Should it then be thus? No, I would tell you what it were to be a judge, and what a prisoner."

"Be content, fair maid!" said Angelo: "it is the law, not I, condemns your brother. Were he my kinsman, my brother, or my son, it should be thus with him. He must die tomorrow."

"Tomorrow?" said Isabel. "Oh, that is sudden: spare him, spare him; he is not prepared for death. Even for our kitchens we kill the fowl in season; shall we serve Heaven with less respect than we minister to our gross selves? Good, good, my lord, bethink you, none have died for my brother's offense, though many have committed it. So you would be the first that gives this sentence, and he the first that suffers it. Go to your own bosom, my lord; knock there, and ask your heart what it does know that is like my brother's fault; if it confess a natural guiltiness such as his is, let it not sound a thought against my brother's life!"

Her last words more moved Angelo than all she had before said, for the beauty of Isabel had raised a guilty passion in his heart, and he began to form thoughts of dishonourable love, such as Claudio's crime had been; and the conflict in his mind made him to turn away from Isabel; but she called him back, saying, "Gentle my lord, turn back; hark[22], how I will bribe you. Good my lord, turn back!"

"How, bribe me?" said Angelo, astonished that she should think of offering him a bribe.

22 hark [hɑːrk] (v.) 〔文學〕聽

"Ay," said Isabel, "with such gifts that heaven itself shall share with you; not with golden treasures, or those glittering stones, whose price is either rich or poor as fancy values them, but with true prayers that shall be up to heaven before sunrise—prayers from preserved souls, from fasting[23] maids whose minds are dedicated to nothing temporal[24]."

"Well, come to me tomorrow," said Angelo.

And for this short respite[25] of her brother's life, and for this permission that she might be heard again, she left him with the joyful hope that she should at last prevail over his stern nature: and as she went away she said: "Heaven keep your honour safe! Heaven save your honour!" Which when Angelo heard, he said within his heart, "Amen, I would be saved from thee and from thy virtues."

And then, affrighted at his own evil thoughts, he said, "What is this? What is this? Do I love her, that I desire to hear her speak again, and feast upon her eyes? What is it I dream on? The cunning enemy of mankind, to catch a saint, with saints does bait the hook. Never could an immodest woman once stir my temper, but this virtuous woman subdues[26] me quite. Even till now, when men were fond, I smiled and wondered at them."

In the guilty conflict in his mind Angelo suffered more that night than the prisoner he had so severely sentenced; for in the prison Claudio was visited by the good duke, who, in his friar's habit, taught the young man the way to heaven, preaching to him the words of penitence[27] and peace.

But Angelo felt all the pangs of irresolute guilt: now wishing to seduce Isabel from the paths of innocence and honour, and now suffering remorse and horror for a crime as yet but intentional. But in the end his evil thoughts prevailed; and he who had so lately started at the offer of a bribe, resolved to tempt this maiden with so high a bribe, as she might not be able to resist, even with the precious gift of her dear brother's life.

When Isabel came in the morning, Angelo desired she might be admitted alone to his presence: and being there he said to her, if she would yield to him her virgin honour and transgress even as Juliet had done with Claudio, he would give her her brother's life.

---

23 fasting ['fæstɪŋ] 禁食的；齋戒的

24 temporal ['tempərəl] (a.) 世俗的；現世的；非精神生活的

25 respite ['respɪt] (n.) 刑罰或義務之展延；暫緩行刑

26 subdue [səb'du:] (v.) 征服；克服

27 penitence ['penɪtəns] (n.) 懺悔；後悔（所犯之錯或罪）

"For," said he, "I love you, Isabel."

"My brother," said Isabel, "did so love Juliet, and yet you tell me he shall die for it."

"But," said Angelo, "Claudio shall not die, if you will consent to visit me by stealth at night, even as Juliet left her father's house at night to come to Claudio."

Isabel, in amazement at his words, that he should tempt her to the same fault for which he passed sentence upon her brother, said, "I would do as much for my poor brother as for myself; that is, were I under sentence of death, the impression of keen whips[28] I would wear as rubies, and go to my death as to a bed that longing I had been sick for, ere[29] I would yield myself up to this shame." And then she told him, she hoped he only spoke these words to try her virtue.

But he said, "Believe me, on my honour, my words express my purpose."

---

28 whip [wɪp] (n.) 鞭打
29 ere [er] (adv.) 〔舊〕〔法〕〔詩〕在前;在⋯⋯之前

Isabel, angered to the heart to hear him use the word Honour to express such dishonourable purposes; said, "Ha! little honour to be much believed; and most pernicious[30] purpose. I will proclaim thee, Angelo, look for it! Sign me a present pardon for my brother, or I will tell the world aloud what man thou art!"

"Who will believe you, Isabel?" said Angelo; "my unsoiled name, the austereness[31] of my life, my word vouched[32] against yours, will outweigh your accusation. Redeem your brother by yielding to my will, or he shall die tomorrow. As for you, say what you can, my false will overweigh your true story. Answer me tomorrow."

"To whom should I complain? Did I tell this, who would believe me?" said Isabel, as she went towards the dreary prison where her brother was confined[33]. When she arrived there, her brother was in pious conversation with the duke, who in his friar's habit had also visited Juliet and brought both these guilty lovers to a proper sense of their fault; and unhappy Juliet with tears and a true remorse confessed that she was more to blame than Claudio, in that she willingly consented to his dishonourable solicitations.

As Isabel entered the room where Claudio was confined, she said, "Peace be here, grace, and good company!"

"Who is there?" said the disguised duke. "Come in; the wish deserves a welcome."

"My business is a word or two with Claudio," said Isabel.

30　pernicious [pər'nɪʃəs] (a.)（對……）有害的；傷害性的
31　austereness [ɔː'stɪrnɪs] (n.) 嚴肅；樸素
32　vouch [vautʃ] (v.) 斷言；明言；保證；擔保；作證
33　confine [kən'faɪn] (v.) 關起來；禁閉

Then the duke left them together, and desired the provost, who had the charge of the prisoners, to place him where he might overhear their conversation.

"Now, sister, what is the comfort?" said Claudio.

Isabel told him he must prepare for death on the morrow.

"Is there no remedy?" said Claudio.

"Yes, brother," replied Isabel, "there is; but such a one as, if you consented to it would strip your honour from you, and leave you naked."

"Let me know the point," said Claudio.

"Oh, I do fear you, Claudio!" replied his sister; "and I quake, lest you should wish to live, and more respect the trifling term of six or seven winters added to your life, than your perpetual honour! Do you dare to die? The sense of death is most in apprehension[34], and the poor beetle that we tread upon, feels a pang as great as when a giant dies."

---

34 apprehension [ˌæprɪˈhenʃən] (n.) 恐懼；憂慮

"Why do you give me this shame?" said Claudio. "Think you I can fetch a resolution from flowery tenderness? If I must die, I will encounter darkness as a bride, and hug it in my arms."

"There spoke my brother," said Isabel; "there my father's grave did utter forth a voice. Yes, you must die; yet would you think it, Claudio! this outward sainted deputy, if I would yield to him my virgin honour, would grant your life. Oh, were it but my life, I would lay it down for your deliverance as frankly as a pin!"

"Thanks, dear Isabel," said Claudio.

"Be ready to die tomorrow," said Isabel.

"Death is a fearful thing," said Claudio.

"And shamed life a hateful," replied his sister.

But the thoughts of death now overcame the constancy of Claudio's temper, and terrors, such as the guilty only at their deaths do know, assailing[35] him, he cried out, "Sweet sister, let me live! The sin you do to save a brother's life, nature dispenses[36] with the deed so far, that it becomes a virtue."

35 assail [ə'seɪl] (v.) 猛擊；痛擊；困擾
36 dispense [dɪ'spens] (v.) 赦免；寬恕

53 "Oh faithless coward! Oh dishonest wretch[37]!" said Isabel. "Would you preserve your life by your sister's shame? Oh, fie[38], fie, fie! I thought, my brother, you had in you such a mind of honour, that had you twenty heads to render up on twenty blocks, you would have yielded them up all before your sister should stoop to such dishonour."

"Nay, hear me, Isabel!" said Claudio.

But what he would have said in defence of his weakness, in desiring to live by the dishonour of his virtuous sister, was interrupted by the entrance of the duke; who said, "Claudio, I have overheard what has passed between you and your sister. Angelo had never the purpose to corrupt her; what he said, has only been to make trial of her virtue. She having the truth of honour in her, has given him that gracious denial which he is most glad to receive. There is no hope that he will pardon you; therefore pass your hours in prayer, and make ready for death."

37 wretch [retʃ] (n.) 卑鄙的人
38 fie [faɪ] (interj.)〔通常為詼諧語〕呸！

Then Claudio repented of his weakness, and said: "Let me ask my sister's pardon! I am so out of love with life, that I will sue to be rid of it." And Claudio retired, overwhelmed with shame and sorrow for his fault.

The duke being now alone with Isabel, commended her virtuous resolution, saying, "The hand that made you fair, has made you good."

"Oh," said Isabel, "how much is the good duke deceived in Angelo! If ever he return, and I can speak to him, I will discover his government." Isabel knew not that she was even now making the discovery she threatened.

The duke replied, "That shall not be much amiss; yet as the matter now stands, Angelo will repel[39] your accusation; therefore lend an attentive ear to my advisings. I believe that you may most righteously do a poor wronged lady a merited benefit, redeem your brother from the angry law, do no stain to your own most gracious person, and much please the absent duke, if peradventure[40] he shall ever return to have notice of this business."

---

39 repel [rɪˈpel] (v.) 拒絕
40 peradventure [ˌpɜːrədˈventʃər] (adv.)〔古〕或許；萬一

Isabel said, she had a spirit to do anything he desired, provided it was nothing wrong.

"Virtue is bold, and never fearful," said the duke: and then he asked her, if she had ever heard of Mariana, the sister of Frederick, the great soldier who was drowned at sea.

"I have heard of the lady," said Isabel, "and good words went with her name."

"This lady," said the duke, "is the wife of Angelo; but her marriage dowry[41] was on board the vessel in which her brother perished, and mark how heavily this befell to the poor gentlewoman! for, beside the loss of a most noble and renowned brother, who in his love towards her was ever most kind and natural, in the wreck[42] of her fortune she lost the affections of her husband, the well-seeming Angelo; who pretending to discover some dishonour in this honourable lady (though the true cause was the loss of her dowry) left her in her tears, and dried not one of them with his comfort. His unjust unkindness, that in all reason should have quenched[43] her love, has, like an impediment[44] in the current, made it more unruly[45], and Mariana loves her cruel husband with the full continuance of her first affection."

41 dowry ['daʊri] (n.) 嫁妝；陪嫁物

42 wreck [rek] (n.)（尤指船遭受暴風雨襲擊所造成的）船難；失事

43 quench [kwentʃ] (v.) 結束；滅絕（希望）

44 impediment [ɪm'pedɪmənt] (n.) 障礙物；障礙

45 unruly [ʌn'ruːli] (a.) 難控制的

🎧 56 The duke then more plainly unfolded his plan. It was, that Isabel should go to Lord Angelo, and seemingly consent to come to him as he desired at midnight; that by this means she would obtain the promised pardon; and that Mariana should go in her stead to the appointment, and pass herself upon Angelo in the dark for Isabel.

"Nor, gentle daughter," said the feigned friar, "fear you to do this thing; Angelo is her husband, and to bring them thus together is no sin.

Isabel being pleased with this project, departed to do as he directed her; and he went to apprise[46] Mariana of their intention. He had before this time visited this unhappy lady in his assumed character, giving her religious instruction and friendly consolation, at which times he had learned her sad story from her own lips; and now she, looking upon him as a holy man, readily consented to be directed by him in this undertaking.

When Isabel returned from her interview with Angelo, to the house of Mariana, where the duke had appointed her to meet him, he said, "Well met, and in good time; what is the news from this good deputy?"

46 apprise [əˈpraɪz] (v.) 〔正式〕通知；報告

Mariana

Isabel related the manner in which she had settled the affair. "Angelo," said she, "has a garden surrounded with a brick wall, on the western side of which is a vineyard, and to that vineyard is a gate."

And then she showed to the duke and Mariana two keys that Angelo had given her; and she said, "This bigger key opens the vineyard gate; this other a little door which leads from the vineyard to the garden. There I have made my promise at the dead of the night to call upon him, and have got from him his word of assurance for my brother's life. I have taken a due and wary[47] note of the place; and with whispering and most guilty diligence he showed me the way twice over."

"Are there no other tokens agreed upon between you, that Mariana must observe?" said the duke.

"No, none," said Isabel, "only to go when it is dark. I have told him my time can be but short; for I have made him think a servant comes along with me, and that this servant is persuaded I come about my brother."

---

47 wary ['weri] (a.) 小心的；慣於留神可能的危機或困難的

The duke commended her discreet management, and she, turning to Mariana, said, "Little have you to say to Angelo, when you depart from him, but soft and low, remember now my brother!"

Mariana was that night conducted to the appointed place by Isabel, who rejoiced that she had, as she supposed, by this device preserved both her brother's life and her own honour.

But that her brother's life was safe the duke was not well satisfied, and therefore at midnight he again repaired to the prison, and it was well for Claudio that he did so, else would Claudio have that night been beheaded; for soon after the duke entered the prison, an order came from the cruel deputy, commanding that Claudio should be beheaded, and his head sent to him by five o'clock in the morning.

But the duke persuaded the provost to put off the execution of Claudio, and to deceive Angelo, by sending him the head of a man who died that morning in the prison.

And to prevail upon the provost to agree to this, the duke, whom still the provost suspected not to be anything more or greater than he seemed, showed the provost a letter written with the duke's hand, and sealed with his seal, which when the provost saw, he concluded this friar must have some secret order from the absent duke, and therefore he consented to spare Claudio; and he cut off the dead man's head and carried it to Angelo.

Then the duke, in his own name, wrote to Angelo a letter, saying that certain accidents had put a stop to his journey, and that he should be in Vienna by the following morning, requiring Angelo to meet him at the entrance of the city, there to deliver up his authority; and the duke also commanded it to be proclaimed, that if any of his subjects craved redress for injustice, they should exhibit their petitions in the street on his first entrance into the city.

Early in the morning Isabel came to the prison, and the duke, who there awaited her coming, for secret reasons thought it good to tell her that Claudio was beheaded; therefore when Isabel inquired if Angelo had sent the pardon for her brother, he said, "Angelo has released Claudio from this world. His head is off, and sent to the deputy."

The much-grieved sister cried out, "Oh unhappy Claudio, wretched Isabel, injurious world, most wicked Angelo!"

The seeming friar bid her take comfort, and when she was become a little calm, he acquainted her with the near prospect of the duke's return, and told her in what manner she should proceed in preferring her complaint against Angelo; and he bade her not fear if the cause should seem to go against her for a while. Leaving Isabel sufficiently instructed, he next went to Mariana, and gave her counsel in what manner she also should act.

Then the duke laid aside his friar's habit, and in his own royal robes, amid a joyful crowd of his faithful subjects, assembled to greet his arrival, entered the city of Vienna, where he was met by Angelo, who delivered up his authority in the proper form.

And there came Isabel, in the manner of a petitioner for redress, and said, "Justice, most royal duke! I am the sister of one Claudio, who, for the seducing a young maid, was condemned to lose his head. I made my suit to Lord Angelo for my brother's pardon. It were needless to tell your grace how I prayed and kneeled, how he repelled me, and how I replied; for this was of much length. The vile conclusion I now begin with grief and shame to utter. Angelo would not, but by my yielding to his dishonourable love release my brother; and after much debate within myself, my sisterly remorse overcame my virtue, and I did yield to him. But the next morning betimes, Angelo, forfeiting his promise, sent a warrant for my poor brother's head!"

The duke affected[48] to disbelieve her story; and Angelo said that grief for her brother's death, who had suffered by the due course of the law, had disordered her senses.

48 affect [ə'fɛkt] (v.) 佯為；假裝

MARIANA. My husband bids me; now I will unmask.

And now another suitor approached, which was Mariana; and Mariana said, "Noble prince, as there comes light from heaven, and truth from breath, as there is sense in truth and truth in virtue, I am this man's wife, and, my good lord, the words of Isabel are false; for the night she says she was with Angelo, I passed that night with him in the garden-house. As this is true, let me in safety rise, or else forever be fixed here a marble monument."

Then did Isabel appeal for the truth of what she had said to Friar Lodowick, that being the name the duke had assumed in his disguise.

Isabel and Mariana had both obeyed his instructions in what they said, the duke intending that the innocence of Isabel should be plainly proved in that public manner before the whole city of Vienna; but Angelo little thought that it was from such a cause that they thus differed in their story, and he hoped from their contradictory evidence to be able to clear himself from the accusation of Isabel; and he said, assuming the look of offended innocence:

"I did but smile till now; but, good my lord, my patience here is touched, and I perceive these poor, distracted women are but the instruments of some greater one, who sets them on. Let me have way, my lord, to find this practise out."

"Ay, with all my heart," said the duke, "and punish them to the height of your pleasure. You, Lord Escalus, sit with Lord Angelo, lend him your pains to discover this abuse; the friar is sent for that set them on, and when he comes, do with your injuries as may seem best in any chastisement[49]. I for a while will leave you, but stir not you, Lord Angelo, till you have well determined upon this slander[50]."

49 chastisement [tʃæsˈtaɪzmənt] (n.) 懲罰
50 slander [ˈslændər] (n.) 毀謗；毀謗罪

The duke then went away, leaving Angelo well pleased to be deputed judge and umpire in his own cause.

But the duke was absent only while he threw off his royal robes and put on his friar's habit; and in that disguise again he presented himself before Angelo and Escalus: and the good old Escalus, who thought Angelo had been falsely accused, said to the supposed friar, "Come, sir, did you set these women on to slander Lord Angelo?"

He replied, "Where is the duke? It is he who should hear me speak."

Escalus said, "The duke is in us, and we will hear you. Speak justly."

"Boldly, at least," retorted[51] the friar; and then he blamed the duke for leaving the cause of Isabel in the hands of him she had accused, and spoke so freely of many corrupt practises he had observed, while, as he said, he had been a looker-on in Vienna, that Escalus threatened, him with the torture for speaking words against the state, and for censuring the conduct of the duke, and ordered him to be taken away to prison. Then, to the amazement of all present, and to the utter confusion of Angelo, the supposed friar threw off his

172

disguise, and they saw it was the duke himself.

The duke first addressed Isabel. He said to her, "Come hither, Isabel. Your friar is now your prince, but with my habit I have not changed my heart. I am still devoted to your service."

"Oh, give me pardon," said Isabel, "that I, your vassal, have employed and troubled your unknown sovereignty."

He answered that he had most need of forgiveness from her, for not having prevented the death of her brother—for not yet would he tell her that Claudio was living; meaning first to make a further trial of her goodness.

Angelo now knew the duke had been a secret witness of his bad deeds, and be said, "Oh my dread lord, I should be guiltier than my guiltiness, to think I can be undiscernible[52], when I perceive your grace, like power divine, has looked upon my actions. Then, good prince, no longer prolong my shame, but let my trial be my own confession. Immediate sentence and death is all the grace I beg."

51 retort [rɪ'tɔːrt] (v.) (尤指對控訴或挑戰) 立即機智地或憤怒地反駁
52 undiscernible [ˌʌndɪ'sɜːrnɪbəl] (a.) 不受辨明的；不被認清的

62

The duke replied, "Angelo, thy faults are manifest. We do condemn thee to the very block where Claudio stooped to death; and with like haste away with him; and for his possessions, Mariana, we do instate and widow you withal[53], to buy you a better husband."

"Oh my dear lord," said Mariana, "I crave[54] no other, nor no better man!" And then on her knees, even as Isabel had begged the life of Claudio, did this kind wife of an ungrateful husband beg the life of Angelo; and she said, "Gentle my liege[55], O good my lord! Sweet Isabel, take my part! Lend me your knees, and all my life to come I will lend you all my life, to do you service!"

The duke said, "Against all sense you importune[56] her. Should Isabel kneel down to beg for mercy, her brother's ghost would break his paved bed, and take her hence in horror."

Still Mariana said, "Isabel, sweet Isabel, do but kneel by me, hold up your hand, say nothing! I will speak all. They say, best men are moulded out of faults, and for the most part become much the better for being a little bad. So may my husband. Oh, Isabel! will you not lend a knee?"

53 withal [wɪˈðɔːl] (adv.) 〔古〕且；此外
54 crave [kreɪv] (v.) 懇求；渴望
55 liege [liːdʒ] (n.) 君主；王侯
56 importune [ˌɪmpərˈtuːn] (v.) 再三要求；不斷請求

H C Selous

63

The duke then said, "He dies for Claudio."

But much pleased was the good duke, when his own Isabel, from whom he expected all gracious and honourable acts, kneeled down before him, and said, "Most bounteous[57] sir, look, if it please you, on this man condemned, as if my brother lived. I partly think a due sincerity governed his deeds, till he did look on me. Since it is so, let him not die! My brother had but justice, in that he did the thing for which he died."

The duke, as the best reply he could make to this noble petitioner for her enemy's life, sending for Claudio from his prison-house, where he lay doubtful of his destiny, presented to her this lamented brother living; and he said to Isabel, "Give me your hand, Isabel; for your lovely sake I pardon Claudio. Say you will be mine, and he shall be my brother, too."

By this time Lord Angelo perceived he was safe and the duke, observing his eye to brighten up a little, said, "Well, Angelo, look that you love your wife; her worth has obtained your pardon. Joy to you, Mariana! Love her, Angelo! I have confessed her, and know her virtue."

Angelo remembered, when dressed in a little brief authority, how hard his heart had been, and felt how sweet is mercy.

The duke commanded Claudio to marry Juliet, and offered himself again to the acceptance of Isabel, whose virtuous and noble conduct had won her prince's heart.

Isabel, not having taken the veil, was free to marry; and the friendly offices, while hid under the disguise of a humble friar, which the noble duke had done for her, made her with grateful joy accept the honour he offered her; and when she became Duchess of Vienna, the excellent example of the virtuous Isabel worked such a complete reformation among the young ladies of that city, that from that time none ever fell into the transgression of Juliet, the repentant wife of the reformed Claudio. And the mercy-loving duke long reigned with his beloved Isabel, the happiest of husbands and of princes.

57 bounteous ['baʊntiəs] (a.)〔文〕慷慨的；豐富的

《一報還一報》名句選

Isabella   But man, proud man,
Dress'd in a little brief authority,
Most ignorant of what he's most assur'd
His glassy essence.
(II, ii, 117–20)

伊莎貝拉   可是,人,驕傲的人,
掌握到一點點短暫的權威,
就會把自己萬分確定的事忘得一乾二淨——
那就是他玻璃易碎的本質。

(第二幕,第二景,117-20行)

Mariana

The Winter's Tale

冬天的故事

《冬天的故事》導讀

《冬天的故事》寫作年代略早於《暴風雨》，此兩劇同為「浪漫劇」（romance），也有離散重聚、失而復得的主題，照理說彼此具有密切關係，但在初版的莎士比亞全集《第一對開本》（*The First Folio*）裡，《暴風雨》是十四個喜劇裡的第一齣喜劇，《冬天的故事》卻是最後一齣。

浪漫劇的劇情

本劇的故事情節像是不合理的浪漫小說或童話故事，有時空的移轉、季節的交替和摧毀後的復原。全劇明顯劃分為兩大段，前半段敘述隆冬時節的西西里宮廷內，國王雷提斯認定王后荷麥妮與幼時認識的好友波希米亞國王波利茲有染，國王妒火中燒，造成了看似無可挽回的罪惡與悲傷。

後半段的故事發生於十六年之後，在春暖時光的波希米亞鄉間，遭到雷提斯狠心遺棄的女兒帕蒂坦初長成，在因緣際會下，和波利茲的獨子弗羅瑞共譜戀曲。但因為帕蒂坦出身低微，波利茲反對兩人結婚，兩人決定和忠臣卡密羅遠赴西西里。後來在雷提斯的宮裡，帕蒂坦真正的身分於此揭曉，王后荷麥妮也奇蹟似地復活，一家人最終和樂團圓。

嫉妒的愚昧

本劇故事源自略早於莎士比亞的劇作家葛林（Robert Greene）在 1588 年所著的小說《潘多托：時間致勝》（*Pandosto: The Triumph of Time*），故事主旨在表現嫉妒所招致的惡果。《冬天的故事》前半段也具有相同意味。雷提斯懷疑猜忌，雷霆大怒，其內心的複雜糾葛，可與莎士比亞的悲劇角色相提並論。

雷提斯一如莎翁四大悲劇《奧賽羅》（*Othello*）中的奧賽羅，因嫉妒仇恨多年好友，間接害死愛妻，並失去王位繼承人的位置。《冬天的故事》強調的是因愚昧而自我摧殘的悲劇，主人翁因此要長年忍受懊悔與孤獨。

荷麥妮是劇中受苦最多、犧牲最大的角色。雷提斯亂吃飛醋，使她在公眾審判中遭到羞辱、失去心愛的兒子、與女兒分離，最後長期離群索居。劇中年幼的王子公主一死一棄，無辜受害。直到象徵新生與活力的春季來臨，年輕的一代才化悲為喜。

「時間」的概念

在前半部的故事裡，主人翁造成悲劇，後半部的故事就用時間和奇蹟來扳平悲劇。《冬天的故事》反映莎士比亞對「時間」的概念，他認為時間如水，能夠載舟亦能覆舟。時間能夠破壞亦能修復，它可以摧毀一切，也可以揭發真相。這種時間哲學和英國詩人史賓賽（Edmund Spenser, 1552–1599）的觀點相似，也因此可以得知，莎士比亞可能不僅知道史賓賽的作品，還進一步借用了他的概念。

荷麥妮在劇末奇蹟似地復生，令觀眾和讀者大吃一驚，人們以為她早已過世，一如葛林的小說《潘多托：時間致勝》。莎士比亞究竟是在最後一刻才改變心意，決定讓她復活，還是從開始就決定隱瞞觀眾，我們不得而知。但在戲劇史上，自始至終都將觀眾蒙在鼓裡的例子少之又少。

荷麥妮從雕像搖身一變成為真人，對現代的許多讀者和觀眾來說，根本是不可思議。然而在十七世紀初期的舞台上，這卻產生了極大的戲劇效果。荷麥妮解釋，雖然她早已原諒雷提斯，但一直到找回帕蒂坦才決定現身。這種說法顯示她之前活在遙遙無期的等待之中，強化了帕蒂坦出現的奇蹟性。

「天性」與「教養」

帕蒂坦出場時只是個牧羊女，卻因具有皇族血統而儀表出眾。莎士比亞在此又觸及了「自然天性」（nature）和「人為教養」（nurture）的主題。在此劇之後推出的《暴風雨》中，也談到了這個主題，並延續了「天性重於教養」的觀念。

戲劇的演出

此劇與另一齣戲《忠誠的牧羊女》（The Faithful Shepherdess）之間，也有令人莞爾的對比。《忠誠的牧羊女》是由莎士比亞所屬的國王御前劇團（King's Men），在推出此劇前一兩年所製作演出的戲碼，由莎士比亞的接班人弗萊徹（John Fletcher）執筆，但那次的演出大為失敗。

弗萊徹在《忠誠的牧羊女》劇出版時曾為文撰序，說明自己原本打算寫一齣悲喜劇，卻因為內容與觀眾的期望相悖而失敗。觀眾想看到盛大節慶歡欣熱鬧的氣氛，也想看演員穿著牧羊袍，牽著牧羊犬在舞台上活動，說些引人發噱的笑話，但他的劇本裡卻沒有安排這些場景。《冬天的故事》則不然，剪羊毛大會一景就充滿了通俗歡樂的成分，一點也沒有讓觀眾失望。

違反戲劇的三一律

《冬天的故事》於 1623 年首次發行在《第一對開本》中。伊麗莎白時代的占星家賽門·福曼（Simon Forman）在日記中寫道，1611 年 5 月，他在環球劇場觀看了《冬天的故事》，這是該劇演出的最早記錄。

這個劇本在詹姆士王朝時期的演出雖然得到觀眾的肯定，但是嚴肅的批評家卻對此劇大加撻伐。莎士比亞的好友英國作家強生（Ben Jonson, 1572–1637）在 1631 年就說，如同《冬天的故事》，包括《暴風雨》，顛覆所有的或然率和自然法則，讓大自然也不得不畏懼。

十八世紀的英國作家強生（Samuel Johnson, 1709–1784）則認為，《冬天的故事》最大的缺陷在於中間一段長達十六年的空白，違反了戲劇的「三一律」*。

　　* 所謂戲劇三一律是指，戲劇的故事情節，在時間上都
　　　發生在一天之內，地點都在同一個場景，劇情只有一
　　　條主線、一個主題。

寓言的意涵

現代的批評早已不作如此想，而是將焦點放在本劇的象徵性，甚至傾向於將此劇視為寓言。劇中人犯下大錯後獲得寬恕的架構，類似《一報還一報》，因此也有人認為這齣戲帶有基督教的訓示意味。

而前面曾提及過的占師家賽門‧福曼，他在觀賞本劇後似乎很滿意。他巨細靡遺地描述該場表演的每個過程，他表示，劇情雖然十分複雜，卻沒有任何荒謬的場景和缺陷。或許有人會感到好奇，那隻把安提貢拖出場外的熊，到底是真熊還是由演員假扮而成，因為當時的倫敦市內有溫馴的熊，也有凶猛的鬥熊。

時至今日，《冬天的故事》在舞台上的出現次數，雖然不如莎士比亞其他的悲劇或喜劇，卻往往有出乎預料的演出效果。而在莎翁的浪漫劇中，《冬天的故事》的曝光率則是僅次於《暴風雨》。

《冬天的故事》人物表

Leontes　　雷提斯　　西西里國王

Hermione　　荷麥妮　　西西里國的王后

Polixenes　　波利茲　　波希米亞國王，西西里國王
　　　　　　　　　　　　雷提斯自幼便認識的好友

Perdita　　帕蒂坦　　被父親雷提斯狠心遺棄而
　　　　　　　　　　　　流落在外的女兒

Florizel　　弗羅瑞　　波希米亞國王波利茲的獨
　　　　　　　　　　　　子，為追求帕蒂坦，曾化名
　　　　　　　　　　　　多里克

Camillo　　卡密羅　　西西里國王雷提斯的勛爵，
　　　　　　　　　　　　是一位正直的臣子

Mamillius	馬密利	西西里國王雷提斯的年幼兒子，不幸因憂傷而早逝
Paulina	寶琳娜	安提貢之妻，王后荷麥妮的密友
Antigonus	安提貢	西西里勳爵，執行遺棄帕蒂坦的任務後身亡
Emilia	愛蜜莉	在地牢服侍荷麥妮的侍女
Cleomenes	克里歐	雷提斯派去德爾菲的阿波羅廟求神諭的使者
Dion	迪翁	和克里歐一同去德爾菲的阿波羅廟求神諭的使者

The Winter's Tale

Leontes, King of Sicily and his queen, the beautiful and virtuous Hermione, once lived in the greatest harmony together. So happy was Leontes in the love of this excellent lady, that he had no wish ungratified, except that he sometimes desired to see again, and to present to his queen, his old companion and schoolfellow, Polixenes, King of Bohemia.

Leontes and Polixenes were brought up together from their infancy[1], but being, by the death of their fathers, called to reign over their respective kingdoms, they had not met for many years, though they frequently interchanged gifts, letters, and loving embassies.

At length, after repeated invitations, Polixenes came from Bohemia to the Sicilian court, to make his friend Leontes a visit.

1 infancy [ˈɪnfənsi] (n.) 幼年時期

🎧65 At first this visit gave nothing but pleasure to Leontes. He recommended the friend of his youth to the queen's particular attention, and seemed in the presence of his dear friend and old companion to have his felicity[2] quite completed. They talked over old times; their school-days and their youthful pranks[3] were remembered, and recounted to Hermione, who always took a cheerful part in these conversations.

When, after a long stay, Polixenes was preparing to depart, Hermione, at the desire of her husband, joined her entreaties[4] to his that Polixenes would prolong his visit.

And now began this good queen's sorrow; for Polixenes refusing to stay at the request of Leontes, was won over by Hermione's gentle and persuasive words to put off his departure for some weeks longer.

Upon this, although Leontes had so long known the integrity[5] and honourable principles of his friend Polixenes, as well as the excellent disposition[6] of his virtuous queen, he was seized with an ungovernable jealousy.

2 felicity [fɪˈlɪsɪti] (n.) 幸福

3 prank [præŋk] (n.) 惡作劇

4 entreaty [ɪnˈtriːti] (n.) 〔正式〕懇求

5 integrity [ɪnˈtegrəti] (n.) 正直；誠實

6 disposition [ˌdɪspəˈzɪʃən] (n.) 性情；氣質

Every attention Hermione showed to Polixenes, though by her husband's particular desire, and merely to please him, increased the unfortunate king's jealousy; and from being a loving and a true friend, and the best and fondest of husbands, Leontes became suddenly a savage and inhuman monster. Sending for Camillo, one of the lords of his court, and telling him of the suspicion he entertained[7], he commanded him to poison Polixenes.

Camillo was a good man; and he, well knowing that the jealousy of Leontes had not the slightest foundation in truth, instead of poisoning Polixenes, acquainted him with the king his master's orders, and agreed to escape with him out of the Sicilian dominions; and Polixenes, with the assistance of Camillo, arrived safe in his own kingdom of Bohemia, where Camillo lived from that time in the king's court, and became the chief friend and favourite of Polixenes.

The flight of Polixenes enraged[8] the jealous Leontes still more; he went to the queen's apartment, where the good lady was sitting with her little son Mamillius, who was just beginning to tell one of his best stories to amuse his mother, when the king entered, and taking the child away, sent Hermione to prison.

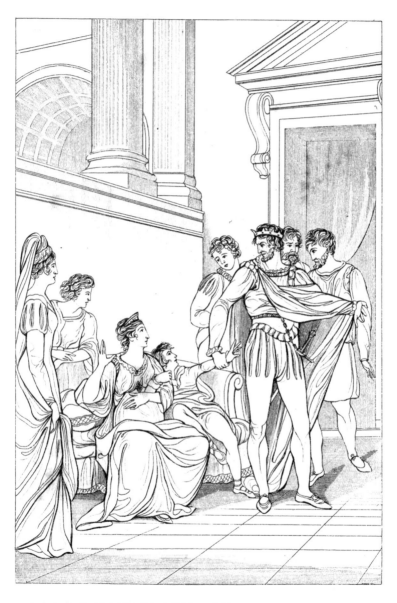

7 entertain [ˌentərˈteɪn] (v.) 懷著；抱著
8 enrage [ɪnˈreɪdʒ] (v.) 激怒

 Mamillius, though but a very young child, loved his mother tenderly; and when he saw her so dishonoured, and found she was taken from him to be put into a prison, he took it deeply to heart, and drooped[9] and pined[10] away by slow degrees, losing his appetite and his sleep, till it was thought his grief would kill him.

The king, when he had sent his queen to prison, commanded Cleomenes and Dion, two Sicilian lords, to go to Delphos, there to inquire of the oracle[11] at the temple of Apollo, if his queen had been unfaithful to him.

When Hermione had been a short time in prison, she was brought to bed of a daughter; and the poor lady received much comfort from the sight of her pretty baby, and she said to it: "My poor little prisoner, I am as innocent as you are."

Hermione had a kind friend in the noble-spirited Paulina, who was the wife of Antigonus, a Sicilian lord and when the lady Paulina heard her royal mistress was brought to bed, she went to the prison where Hermione was confined; and she said to Emilia, a lady who attended upon Hermione, "I pray you, Emilia, tell the good queen, if her majesty dare trust me with her little babe, I will carry it to the king, its father; we do not know how he may soften at the sight of his innocent child."

"Most worthy madam," replied Emilia, "I will acquaint the queen with your noble offer; she was wishing today that she had any friend who would venture to present the child to the king."

"And tell her," said Paulina, "that I will speak boldly to Leontes in her defence."

9 droop [druːp] (v.) 頹喪；委靡不振
10 pine [paɪn] (v.) 消瘦；憔悴
11 oracle [ˈɔːrəkəl] (n.) 神諭

🎧 68 "May you be for ever blessed," said Emilia, "for your kindness to our gracious queen!"

Emilia then went to Hermione, who joyfully gave up her baby to the care of Paulina, for she had feared that no one would dare venture to present the child to its father.

Paulina took the newborn infant, and forcing herself into the king's presence, notwithstanding her husband, fearing the king's anger, endeavoured to prevent her, she laid the babe at its father's feet, and Paulina made a noble speech to the king in defence of Hermione, and she reproached[12] him severely for his inhumanity, and implored him to have mercy on his innocent wife and child.

But Paulina's spirited remonstrances[13] only aggravated[14] Leontes' displeasure, and he ordered her husband Antigonus to take her from his presence.

When Paulina went away, she left the little baby at its father's feet, thinking when he was alone with it, he would look upon it, and have pity on its helpless innocence.

12 reproach [rɪˈprəʊtʃ] (v.) 責備
13 remonstrance [rɪˈmɑːnstrəns] (n.) 抗議
14 aggravate [ˈægrəveɪt] (v.) 使惡化

The good Paulina was mistaken: for no sooner was she gone than the merciless father ordered Antigonus, Paulina's husband, to take the child, and carry it out to sea, and leave it upon some desert shore to perish.

Antigonus, unlike the good Camillo, too well obeyed the orders of Leontes; for he immediately carried the child on shipboard, and put out to sea, intending to leave it on the first desert coast he could find.

So firmly was the king persuaded of the guilt of Hermione, that he would not wait for the return of

Cleomenes and Dion, whom he had sent to consult the oracle of Apollo at Delphos, but before the queen was recovered from her lying-in[15], and from her grief for the loss of her precious baby, he had her brought to a public trial before all the lords and nobles of his court.

And when all the great lords, the judges, and all the nobility of the land were assembled together to try Hermione, and that unhappy queen was standing as a prisoner before her subjects[16] to receive their judgement Cleomenes and Dion entered the assembly, and presented to the king the answer of the oracle, sealed up; and Leontes commanded the seal to be broken, and the words of the oracle to be read aloud, and these were the words:

"Hermione is innocent,
Polixenes blameless,
Camillo a true subject,
Leontes a jealous tyrant,
and the king shall live without an heir
if that which is lost be not found."

---

15 lying-in (n.) 分娩
16 subject ['sʌbdʒɪkt] (n.) 庶民；子民

🎧 70 The king would give no credit to the words of the oracle: he said it was a falsehood invented by the queen's friends, and he desired the judge to proceed in the trial of the queen; but while Leontes was speaking, a man entered and told him that the Prince Mamillius, hearing his mother was to be tried for her life, struck with grief and shame, had suddenly died.

Hermione, upon hearing of the death of this dear affectionate[17] child, who had lost his life in sorrowing for her misfortune, fainted; and Leontes, pierced[18] to the heart by the news, began to feel pity for his unhappy queen, and he ordered Paulina, and the ladies who were her attendants, to take her away, and use means for her recovery.

Paulina soon returned, and told the king that Hermione was dead.

When Leontes heard that the queen was dead, he repented of his cruelty to her; and now that he thought his ill-usage had broken Hermione's heart, he believed her innocent; and now he thought the words of the oracle were true, as he knew "if that which was lost was not found," which he concluded was his young daughter, he should be without an heir, the young Prince Mamillius being dead; and he would give his kingdom now to recover his lost daughter: and Leontes gave himself up to remorse[19], and passed many years in mournful thoughts and repentant grief.

The ship in which Antigonus carried the infant princess out to sea was driven by a storm upon the coast of Bohemia, the very kingdom of the good King Polixenes. Here Antigonus landed, and here he left the little baby.

Antigonus never returned to Sicily to tell Leontes where he had left his daughter, for as he was going back to the ship, a bear came out of the woods, and tore him to pieces; a just punishment on him for obeying the wicked order of Leontes.

17　affectionate [əˈfekʃənət] (a.) 摯愛的
18　pierce [pɪrs] (v.) 深深地打動
19　remorse [rɪˈmɔːrs] (n.) 懊悔；悔恨

🎧 71 ▸ The child was dressed in rich clothes and jewels; for Hermione had made it very fine when she sent it to Leontes, and Antigonus had pinned a paper to its mantle[20], and the name of *Perdita* written thereon, and words obscurely intimating[21] its high birth and untoward[22] fate.

This poor deserted baby was found by a shepherd. He was a humane man, and so he carried the little Perdita home to his wife, who nursed it tenderly; but poverty tempted[23] the shepherd to conceal[24] the rich prize he had found: therefore he left that part of the country, that no one might know where he got his riches, and with part of Perdita's jewels he bought herds of sheep, and became a wealthy shepherd.

He brought up Perdita as his own child, and she knew not she was any other than a shepherd's daughter.

The little Perdita grew up a lovely maiden; and though she had no better education than that of a shepherd's daughter, yet so did the natural graces she inherited from her royal mother shine forth in her untutored mind, that no one from her behaviour would have known she had not been brought up in her father's court.

20 mantle ['mæntl] (n.) 斗篷
21 intimate ['ɪntɪmət] (v.) 提示；暗示
22 untoward [ˌʌntə'wɔːrd] (a.) 不幸的
23 tempt ['tempt] (v.) 誘惑
24 conceal [kən'siːl] (v.) 隱藏；隱瞞

🎧72 Polixenes, the King of Bohemia, had an only son, whose name was Florizel. As this young prince was hunting near the shepherd's dwelling, he saw the old man's supposed daughter; and the beauty, modesty, and queen-like deportment[25] of Perdita caused him instantly to fall in love with her.

He soon, under the name of Doricles, and in the disguise of a private gentleman, became a constant visitor at the old shepherd's house. Florizel's frequent absences from court alarmed Polixenes; and setting people to watch his son, he discovered his love for the shepherd's fair daughter.

Polixenes then called for Camillo, the faithful Camillo, who had preserved his life from the fury of Leontes, and desired that he would accompany him to the house of the shepherd, the supposed father of Perdita.

Polixenes and Camillo, both in disguise, arrived at the old shepherd's dwelling while they were celebrating the feast of sheepshearing; and though they were strangers, yet at the sheepshearing every guest being made welcome, they were invited to walk in, and join in the general festivity.

25 deportment [dɪˈpɔːrtmənt] (n.) 行為；舉止

Nothing but mirth[26] and jollity[27] was going forward. Tables were spread, and great preparations were making for the rustic feast. Some lads and lasses were dancing on the green before the house, while others of the young men were buying ribands[28], gloves, and such toys, of a pedlar at the door.

While this busy scene was going forward, Florizel and Perdita sat quietly in a retired corner, seemingly more pleased with the conversation of each other, than desirous of engaging in the sports and silly amusements of those around them.

The king was so disguised that it was impossible his son could know him: he therefore advanced near enough to hear the conversation. The simple yet elegant manner in which Perdita conversed with his son did not a little surprise Polixenes: he said to Camillo: "This is the prettiest low-born lass I ever saw; nothing she does or says but looks like something greater than herself, too noble for this place."

Camillo replied: "Indeed she is the very queen of curds[29] and cream."

"Pray, my good friend," said the king to the old shepherd," what fair swain[30] is that talking with your daughter?"

26　mirth [mɜːrθ] (n.) 歡樂
27　jollity [ˈdʒɑːlɪti] (n.) 愉快
28　riband [ˈrɪbənd] (n.) 〔古〕飾帶（同 ribbon）
29　curd [kɜːrd] (n.) 凝乳（牛奶變酸時的凝結物，可用來製作乳酪）
30　swain [sweɪn] (n.) 戀愛中的青年（特指仰慕者或情人）

"They call him Doricles," replied the shepherd. "He says he loves my daughter; and, to speak truth, there is not a kiss to choose which loves the other best. If young Doricles can get her, she shall bring him that he little dreams of"; meaning the remainder of Perdita's jewels; which, after he had bought herds of sheep with part of them, he had carefully hoarded up for her marriage portion.

Polixenes then addressed his son. "How now, young man!" said he: "your heart seems full of something that takes off your mind from feasting. When I was young, I used to load my love with presents; but you have let the pedlar go and have bought your lass no toy."

The young prince, who little thought he was talking to the king his father, replied, "Old sir, she prizes not such trifles; the gifts which Perdita expects from me are locked up in my heart."

Then turning to Perdita, he said to her, "O hear me, Perdita, before this ancient gentleman, who it seems was once himself a lover; he shall hear what I profess."

Florizel then called upon the old stranger to be a witness to a solemn promise of marriage which he made to Perdita, saying to Polixenes, "I pray you, mark our contract."

"Mark your divorce, young sir," said the king, discovering himself.

Polixenes then reproached his son for daring to contract himself to this low-born maiden, calling Perdita "shepherd's brat[31], sheep-hook," and other disrespectful names; and threatening, if ever she suffered his son to see her again, he would put her, and the old shepherd her father, to a cruel death.

The king then left them in great wrath[32], and ordered Camillo to follow him with Prince Florizel.

When the king had departed, Perdita, whose royal nature was roused by Polixenes' reproaches, said, "Though we are all undone, I was not much afraid; and once or twice I was about to speak, and tell him plainly that the selfsame sun which shines upon his palace, hides not his face from our cottage, but looks on both alike."

Then sorrowfully she said: "But now I am awakened from this dream, I will queen it no further. Leave me, sir; I will go milk my ewes[33] and weep."

31 brat [bræt] (n.) 〔貶〕小兒
32 wrath [ræθ] (n.) 〔文〕盛怒
33 ewe [ju:] (n.) 母羊

The kind-hearted Camillo was charmed with the spirit and propriety[34] of Perdita's behaviour; and perceiving that the young prince was too deeply in love to give up his mistress at the command of his royal father, he thought of a way to befriend the lovers, and at the same time to execute a favourite scheme he had in his mind.

Camillo had long known that Leontes, the King of Sicily, was become a true penitent[35]; and though Camillo was now the favoured friend of King Polixenes, he could not help wishing once more to see his late royal master and his native home. He therefore proposed to Florizel and Perdita that they should accompany him to the Sicilian court, where he would engage Leontes should protect them till, through his mediation, they could obtain pardon from Polixenes, and his consent to their marriage.

To this proposal they joyfully agreed; and Camillo, who conducted everything relative to their flight[36], allowed the old shepherd to go along with them.

34 propriety [prə'praɪəti] (n.) 〔正式〕行為得體；禮貌
35 penitent ['penɪtənt] (n.) 悔過者
36 flight [flaɪt] (n.) 逃亡

The shepherd took with him the remainder of Perdita's jewels, her baby clothes, and the paper which he had found pinned to her mantle.

After a prosperous voyage, Florizel and Perdita, Camillo and the old shepherd, arrived in safety at the court of Leontes. Leontes, who still mourned his dead Hermione and his lost child, received Camillo with great kindness, and gave a cordial[37] welcome to Prince Florizel.

But Perdita, whom Florizel introduced as his princess, seemed to engross[38] all Leontes' attention: perceiving a resemblance between her and his dead queen Hermione, his grief broke out afresh, and he said, such a lovely creature might his own daughter have been, if he had not so cruelly destroyed her.

"And then, too," said he to Florizel, "I lost the society and friendship of your grave father, whom I now desire more than my life once again to look upon."

---

37 cordial ['kɔːrdʒəl] (a.) 衷心的；真摯的
38 engross [ɪn'groʊs] (v.) 使全神貫注

🎧 78 When the old shepherd heard how much notice the king had taken of Perdita, and that he had lost a daughter, who was exposed in infancy, he fell to comparing the time when he found the little Perdita, with the manner of its exposure, the jewels and other tokens of its high birth; from all which it was impossible for him not to conclude that Perdita and the king's lost daughter were the same.

Florizel and Perdita, Camillo and the faithful Paulina, were present when the old shepherd related to the king the manner in which he had found the child, and also the circumstance of Antigonus' death, he having seen the bear seize upon him.

He showed the rich mantle in which Paulina remembered Hermione had wrapped the child; and he produced a jewel which she remembered Hermione had tied about Perdita's neck, and he gave up the paper which Paulina knew to be the writing of her husband; it could not be doubted that Perdita was Leontes' own daughter: but oh! the noble struggles of Paulina, between sorrow for her husband's death, and joy that the oracle was fulfilled, in the king's heir, his long-lost daughter being found.

When Leontes heard that Perdita was his daughter, the great sorrow that he felt that Hermione was not living to behold[39] her child, made him that he could say nothing for a long time, but "O thy mother, thy mother!"

39 behold [bɪˈhoʊld] (v.) 〔舊〕〔文〕看見;看

Paulina interrupted this joyful yet distressful scene, with saying to Leontes, that she had a statue newly finished by that rare Italian master, Julio Romano, which was such a perfect resemblance of the queen, that would his majesty be pleased to go to her house and look upon it, he would be almost ready to think it was Hermione herself. Thither[40] then they all went; the king anxious to see the semblance of his Hermione, and Perdita longing to behold what the mother she never saw did look like.

When Paulina drew back the curtain which concealed this famous statue, so perfectly did it resemble Hermione, that all the king's sorrow was renewed at the sight: for a long time he had no power to speak or move.

"I like your silence, my liege[41]," said Paulina, "it the more shows your wonder. Is not this statue very like your queen?"

At length the king said: "O, thus she stood, even with such majesty, when I first wooed her. But yet, Paulina, Hermione was not so aged as this statue looks."

Paulina replied: "So much the more the carver's excellence, who has made the statue as Hermione would have looked had she been living now. But let me draw the curtain, sire[42], lest presently you think it moves."

40 thither ['θɪðər] (adv.) 到彼處
41 liege [liːdʒ] (n.) 君主；王侯
42 sire [saɪr] (n.)〔舊〕對國王或皇帝的敬稱

The king then said: "Do not draw the curtain, Would I were dead! See, Camillo, would you not think it breathed? Her eye seems to have motion in it."

"I must draw the curtain, my liege," said Paulina. "You are so transported[43], you will persuade yourself the statue lives."

"O, sweet Paulina," said Leontes, "make me think so twenty years together! Still methinks[44] there is an air comes from her. What fine chisel[45] could ever yet cut breath? Let no man mock me, for I will kiss her."

"Good my lord, forbear[46]!" said Paulina. "The ruddiness upon her lip is wet; you will stain your own with oily painting. Shall I draw the curtain?"

"No, not these twenty years," said Leontes.

Perdita, who all this time had been kneeling, and beholding in silent admiration the statue of her matchless mother, said now, "And so long could I stay here, looking upon my dear mother."

"Either forbear this transport," said Paulina to Leontes, "and let me draw the curtain; or prepare yourself for more amazement. I can make the statue move indeed; ay, and descend from off the pedestal[47], and take you by the hand. But then you will think, which I protest I am not, that I am assisted by some wicked powers."

43 transport ['trænspɔːrt] (v.) 〔文〕使忘我；使激動
44 methinks [mɪ'θɪŋks] (v.) 〔古〕據我看來
45 chisel ['tʃɪzəl] (n.) 鑿子
46 forbear ['fɔːrber] (v.) 〔正式〕自制；忍耐
47 pedestal ['pedɪstəl] (n.) 臺座；塑像的墊座

"What you can make her do," said the astonished king, "I am content to look upon. What you can make her speak, I am content to hear; for it is as easy to make her speak as move."

Paulina then ordered some slow and solemn music, which she had prepared for the purpose, to strike up; and, to the amazement of all the beholders, the statue came down from off the pedestal, and threw its arms around Leontes' neck. The statue then began to speak, praying for blessings on her husband, and on her child, the newly-found Perdita.

No wonder that the statue hung upon Leontes' neck, and blessed her husband and her child. No wonder; for the statue was indeed Hermione herself, the real, the living queen.

Paulina had falsely reported to the king the death of Hermione, thinking that the only means to preserve her royal mistress' life; and with the good Paulina, Hermione had lived ever since, never choosing Leontes should know she was living, till she heard Perdita was found; for though she had long forgiven the injuries which Leontes had done to herself, she could not pardon his cruelty to his infant daughter.

His dead queen thus restored to life, his lost daughter found, the long-sorrowing Leontes could scarcely support the excess of his own happiness.

Nothing but congratulations and affectionate speeches were heard on all sides. Now the delighted parents thanked Prince Florizel for loving their lowlyseeming daughter; and now they blessed the good old shepherd for preserving their child. Greatly did Camillo and Paulina rejoice that they had lived to see so good an end of all their faithful services.

And as if nothing should be wanting to complete this strange and unlooked-for joy, King Polixenes himself now entered the palace.

When Polixenes first missed his son and Camillo, knowing that Camillo had long wished to return to Sicily, he conjectured[48] he should find the fugitives[49] here; and, following them with all speed, he happened to just arrive at this, the happiest moment of Leontes' life.

48 conjecture [kən'dʒektʃər] (v.) 猜測；推測
49 fugitive ['fjuːdʒɪtɪv] (n.) 逃亡者；逃犯

Polixenes took a part in the general joy; he forgave his friend Leontes the unjust jealousy he had conceived against him, and they once more loved each other with all the warmth of their first boyish friendship. And there was no fear that Polixenes would now oppose his son's marriage with Perdita. She was no "sheep-hook" now, but the heiress of the crown of Sicily.

Thus have we seen the patient virtues of the long-suffering Hermione rewarded. That excellent lady lived many years with her Leontes and her Perdita, the happiest of mothers and of queens.

《冬天的故事》名句選

Polixenes   We were as twinn'd lambs that did frisk i'the sun,
                  And bleat the one at the other: what we chang'd
                  Was innocence for innocence; we knew not
                  The doctrine of ill-doing, no, nor dream'd
                  That any did.
                  (Act 1, scene 2, lines 67–71)

波利茲   我們猶如在陽光下歡躍的一對孿生羔羊，
           彼此交換著咩咩的叫喚：
           我們以一片天真，與對方相待，
           我們不懂得作惡，
           也不曾想過人世間裡會有人行惡事。
           （第一幕，第二景，67–71 行）

Shepherd   I think there is not half a kiss to choose
Who loves another best.
(IV, iii, 175–176)

牧羊人   我想沒有半個吻能看得出誰愛誰多。
（第四幕，第三景，175–176 行）

Perdita   The selfsame sun that shines upon his court
Hides not his visage from our cottage, but
Looks on alike.
(IV, iii, 448–50)

帕蒂坦   照耀他的皇宮的那個太陽，
不對我們的村莊隱其光芒，而是
一視同仁。
（第四幕，第三景，448–50 行）

馴悍記

P. 26 　　凱瑟琳是帕都亞一位富紳巴提塔的長女。這位姑娘特別難管教，她脾氣暴躁，罵起人來，嗓門特別大，所以帕都亞的居民都稱她是「潑婦凱瑟琳」。

　　要找個紳士冒險來娶這位姑娘，大概難如登天。巴提塔也收到了不少的埋怨，因為很多傑出的青年來向溫柔的妹妹碧安卡求婚，可是巴提塔不肯答應。他再三延緩，老是藉口推託說，等長女出閣了，才會輪到年紀較小的碧安卡。

P. 28 　　這時，有位叫作皮楚丘的紳士，正好特地來帕都亞物色妻子。凱瑟琳傳言中的脾氣，並沒有讓他退卻。他一聽說凱瑟琳多金又美麗，便決定要娶這位出名的潑婦，再把她調教成一位溫順聽話的妻子。

　　的確，再沒有人比皮楚丘更能勝任這項艱難的任務了。皮楚丘的個性和凱瑟琳一樣強硬，可是他也是個機智快活的開心果，充滿智慧，善於判斷。他個性從容自在，在心情很平靜時，也可以裝出一副激

動生氣的樣子，然後暗地裡為
自己佯裝出的憤怒開心大笑。

　　像這樣的人要是當了凱瑟
琳的丈夫，就有能耐把佯裝粗
暴當成是一種消遣。但嚴格說
來，這應該算是拜他高明的洞
察力所賜，因為要對付凱瑟琳
的壞脾氣，唯一的辦法就是以
其人之道還治其人之身。

P. 30　　皮楚丘前來向潑婦凱瑟琳
求婚，他請她父親巴提塔允許

Petruchio

他追求他的「溫順女兒」凱瑟琳。皮楚丘這麼稱呼她，還俏皮
地說，聽說她性格靦腆，舉止溫順，所以他就特地從維洛那城
來這裡向她求婚。

　　她父親是很希望把她嫁出去，但也不得不承認凱瑟琳的
個性並非如此。她能有多溫柔，一下子就見真章，因為她的音
樂老師正衝進門來，抱怨他的學生「溫順的凱瑟琳」剛剛用魯
特琴打破他的頭，因為他竟敢挑剔她彈琴的毛病。聽他這麼一
講，皮楚丘說道：「好個勇猛的姑娘呀，這一下她更令我著迷
了，我想和她聊聊。」

　　便催促老先生給他一個確定的答案，他表示：「巴提塔先
生，我的生意繁忙，可不能每天都來求婚。您知道我的父親已
經歸天，他留下土地產業讓我繼承。請您告訴我，我要是得到
了令媛的芳心，您打算給她什麼嫁妝？」

P. 32　　巴提塔雖覺得這位提親者的態度有些魯莽，但也很高興能
把凱瑟琳嫁出去。他回答會給她兩萬克朗作為嫁妝，而且在他

死後還可以得到一半的地產。於是，這樁莫名其妙的婚事就這樣敲定了。巴提塔去找潑辣的女兒，表示有人來提親，要她去皮楚丘的面前接受求婚。

　　同一時間，皮楚丘琢磨著該用何種方式來求婚。他說：「等她來了，我要神采奕奕地向她求婚。她要是罵我，那我就說她的歌聲美若夜鶯。她要是對我皺眉頭，我就說她像帶露的玫瑰一樣清新。她要是半句話也不吭，我就讚美她能言善道。她要是叫我離開，我就跟她道謝，就好像是她留我住一個星期一樣。」

　　神氣威風的凱瑟琳這時走了進來。皮楚丘對她說：「早啊，『凱特』，聽說這是妳的芳名吧。」

P.34　　這種簡稱讓凱瑟琳很反感，她輕蔑地說：「別人跟我說話時，都叫我『凱瑟琳』。」

　　「妳騙我，妳就叫『大剌剌凱特』，也叫『俏凱特』，有時又叫『潑婦凱特』。但是凱特啊，妳是天底下最美麗的凱特，所以凱特啊，一聽到每個地方的人都讚美妳的溫和柔順，我就前來向妳求婚，請妳做我的妻子。」提親者答道。

這是一場古怪的求婚，凱瑟琳氣沖沖地吼說，要讓他知道她這潑婦之名當之無愧，而他卻自顧自地讚美她說話又甜又有禮貌，直到最後皮楚丘聽到她父親走來，他就說（為了盡快完成求婚）：「『甜心凱瑟琳』，我們就暫且不再閒聊了。妳父親已經答應把妳嫁給我，嫁妝也已經談妥，不管妳願不願意，我都要娶妳。」

這時巴提塔走進門，皮楚丘告訴他，他女兒殷勤地接待他，還答應下星期日就結婚。凱瑟琳否認他所說的話，還表示寧願在星期天看到他被吊死，接著又怪父親竟要她嫁給皮楚丘這樣一個發神經的無賴。

P. 36　　皮楚丘請她父親不要把她的氣話當真，因為他們已經講好，她在父親面前要表現出拒抗的樣子，但在私底下相處時，他知道她是非常溫柔多情的女子。他對她說：「凱特，把你的手給我，我要去威尼斯為妳買些結婚當天要穿的漂亮禮服。岳父，請您準備喜宴，邀請客人來參加婚禮吧。我一定會把戒指和錦衣繡服都準備好，讓我的凱瑟琳一身光鮮。吻我吧，凱特，我們星期天就要結婚了。」

星期天時，參加婚禮的客人都到齊了，可是等了老半天，還不見皮楚丘出現，讓凱瑟琳氣得都哭了，覺得皮楚丘不過是在耍著她玩。

　　最後，皮楚丘終於出現。然而，他不但沒有帶上原本說好要給凱瑟琳的新娘禮服，連他自己也穿得不像個新郎，一身古里古怪又亂七八糟，好像存心來這個正式的典禮上鬧場。他的僕人和座騎，也是一樣寒傖古怪。

P. 38　　大家怎麼勸皮楚丘，他就是不肯換套衣服。他說，凱瑟琳要嫁的是他的人，又不是他的衣服。人們勸不動他，只好將就著進教堂。他從頭到尾一副瘋瘋癲癲的樣子，牧師問皮楚丘願不願意娶凱瑟琳為妻，他回答願意的音量之大，嚇得牧師連書本都掉落在地上。當牧師彎下腰去撿書時，裝瘋賣傻的新郎又捶了他一下，把牧師和書本都打到地上，現場一片驚訝。

　　整個婚禮上，皮楚丘一直又踩腳又喊叫，連大膽的凱瑟琳也被嚇得打哆嗦。婚禮結束後，他們還未走出教堂時，皮楚丘就吩咐拿酒來，扯大嗓門向眾人敬酒，還把他泡在杯底的麵包，往教堂司事的臉上扔過去。對這個奇怪的舉動，他只解釋說，司事的鬍子長得很稀疏，一副餓相，好像在跟他討他泡著喝的那塊麵包。

P. 40 　　這真是前所未見的烏龍婚禮，不過皮楚丘這些瘋瘋癲癲的行為都是裝出來的，這樣才能利於馴悍妻計畫的進行。

　　巴提塔辦了一場豪華筵宴，當他們從教堂回來時，皮楚丘一把抓住凱瑟琳，表示立刻就要帶妻子回家。岳父跟他抗議，發火的凱瑟琳滿口怒言，但他還是執意要這麼做。他表示，做丈夫的有權隨意處置妻子，接著就趕凱瑟琳上路。他一副天不怕地不怕、吃了秤砣鐵了心的樣子，誰也不敢攔他。

　　皮楚丘故意挑選一匹乾癟瘦弱的馬讓妻子乘坐，而他和僕人的馬也好不到哪裡去。他們走的路坑坑洞洞，泥濘不堪。要是凱瑟琳的馬累得走不動而絆倒時，皮楚丘就大發雷霆，臭罵那頭可憐又精疲力盡的牲畜，他看起來就像是天底下最火爆的人。

P. 42 　　在一段折騰人的路程之後，他們終於到了皮楚丘的家。這一路上，凱瑟琳只聽得皮楚丘對僕人和馬匹滿口咒罵。

　　皮楚丘親切地歡迎她回家，但決定讓她當天晚上既不能睡覺，也不能吃東西。餐桌鋪好之後，晚餐很快就端上了，可是

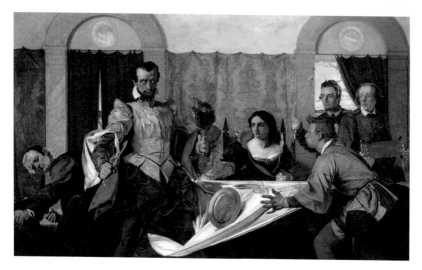

皮楚丘對每一道菜都挑毛病，還把肉扔到地上，命令僕人把晚餐端下去。他表示，他這樣做都是為了他愛的凱瑟琳，為了不讓她吃到烹調差勁的食物。

當又累又沒吃飯的凱瑟琳想要休息時，他又開始挑剔起床鋪，把枕頭和被單丟得整個房間都是，讓她只得坐在椅子上。她只要一打盹，馬上就被丈夫的大嗓門給吵醒，聽他吼罵那些僕人沒有把他妻子的新婚床鋪打點好。

翌日，皮楚丘故計重施。他跟凱瑟琳講話時仍舊客客氣氣，可是當她想吃飯時，他又對每樣端到她面前的東西挑三揀四。跟昨晚的晚餐一樣，他把早餐丟到地上。驕傲的凱瑟琳呀，她這下也不得不偷偷求僕人給她點東西吃了。不過僕人都有皮楚丘的命令在先，不敢背著主人給她東西吃。

P. 44 她說：「啊，他娶我是為了餓死我嗎？乞丐晃到我娘家門口，都還可以討到東西吃。而我呢，從來也沒向人討過東西的人，現在卻落得沒得吃沒得睡，肚子又餓，頭又暈。他大吵大罵，吵得我睡不著，耳邊都是他的叫罵聲。最氣人的是，他還

說是為了愛我才這樣做，好像是我只要睡了、吃了，就馬上會死掉似的。」

這時皮楚丘走進門，打斷她這番喃喃自語。他並不想餓壞她，而是給她帶來了些食物，然後問道：「我親愛的凱特還好嗎？愛人啊，妳看，我可是很用心的，這是我親自為你做的菜，我相信妳一定會很感動。怎麼不講話？妳不喜歡這些飯菜？那算我白費一場囉。」

他接著命令僕人把盤子端走。凱瑟琳飢腸轆轆，銳氣盡失，所以儘管一肚子氣，她還是說：「就請你把它留下吧。」

P. 46　但皮楚丘對她的要求還不只這些，他說：「服務再差，好歹也得道個謝。所以啊，在妳開動之前，也該謝謝我一聲才對。」

凱瑟琳只得心不甘情不願地說：「先生，謝謝。」

他現在終於讓她吃點東西了。他說：「凱特，吃點東西對妳的溫順性情會有幫助。我的甜心，快點吃吧！我們要回岳父家了，你要打扮得體面一點，穿上絲衣緞帽，戴上金戒指，加上縐領，披上圍巾，帶上扇子，什麼都要準備個兩套替換。」

P. 47　皮楚丘為了讓她相信他真的會為她準備這些行頭，他叫來裁縫師和帽匠，而他們也把皮楚丘為她挑選的新衣服都帶來。不等她吃個半飽，皮楚丘就叫人把她的盤子收走，說道：「怎麼樣了，妳吃完了吧？」

帽匠拿出一頂帽子，說：「這就是閣下訂的帽子。」皮楚丘看了又開始破口大罵，說那頂帽子的形狀像個湯杯，大小跟蛤蜊或胡桃殼一樣大，要帽匠拿回去再做大一點。

　　凱瑟琳說：「就這頂了，名媛淑女都戴這種帽子的。」

　　皮楚丘回答：「等妳成為名媛淑女時，妳就會有一頂了，現在還不行。」

P. 48　　剛吃過點肉之後，凱瑟琳不再那麼精神不濟。她說：「噢，先生，我相信我也有權利說話，我就是要說：我不是嬰兒或三歲小孩了！你最好耐著性子聽我講話，如果你聽不下去，就把你的耳朵塞起來吧。」

　　皮楚丘不理會她的這些氣話。他很高興找到了好方法來管教妻子，而不用跟她大吵大鬧。他回答：「哎，妳說得對。這帽子多彆腳啊，我就愛妳看不上它。」

　　「你愛不愛我都無所謂。我看上這頂帽子，我就只要這頂，其他的都不要。」凱瑟琳說。

　　「妳說妳想看看禮服。」皮楚丘說著，假裝聽錯她的話。

　　裁縫師走過來，拿來一件為她做的精美禮服。皮楚丘打算讓她拿不到帽子和禮服，所以又開始挑毛病。

P. 49　　「哦，拜託，天啊！這是什麼鳥玩意！你說這是袖子？根本就像半個炮筒嘛，又像蘋果派一樣，一層一層的。」他說。

240

裁縫師說：「您吩咐過我要根據最新的流行款式來做。」凱瑟琳也表示，這是她見過最時髦漂亮的禮服了。

P. 50　　皮楚丘覺得鬧到這樣也夠了。他私下吩咐，一定要付錢給裁縫師和帽商，並向他們致歉自己的態度很莫名其妙。他講話粗暴，氣呼呼地把裁縫和帽商趕出房間，然後轉身向凱瑟琳說：「好吧，我的凱特，走吧，我們還是穿現在穿的普通衣服去岳父家吧。」

之後他叫人備馬，並表示現在才七點，一定要在午飯時間趕到巴提塔家。但事實上他說這話時，早已不是一大清早，而是中午時分了。皮楚丘的火爆舉止差不多已經制服了凱瑟琳，讓她只得謙恭地說：「先生，容我告訴你，現在已經兩點了，我們連晚餐都會趕不上。」

但皮楚丘準備在去岳父家之前，把她調教但百依百順，讓她不管他說什麼，都會言聽計從。因此，他就一副連太陽和時間都能操控的樣子，表示他高興說幾點就是幾點，要不然他就不去了。他說：「不管我說什麼、做什麼，妳都跟我唱反調，所以我今天不走了。如果我要走，我說幾點就是幾點。」

P. 52　　隔天，凱瑟琳只得力行她新學到的服從。皮楚丘要等到把她的傲氣完全馴服，連「反駁」這種字眼想都不敢想時，才准她回娘家。然而，即使都上路了，他們還險些半路折返，因為皮楚丘說「日中月亮高照」時，她不經意地表示了是「太陽、不是月亮」。

「現在，以吾母之子起誓。也就是，用我這個人來起誓，我說月亮就是月亮，我說星星就是星星，我說什麼就是什麼，要不然就不去岳父家。」他說。

說完他就作勢又要折返，但這時的凱瑟琳已不再是「潑婦凱瑟琳」，而是一個百依百順的妻子。她說：「我們都走這麼遠了，就求你繼續走吧。太陽或月亮都好，你說什麼就是什麼，你高興叫它是燈芯草蠟燭也行，我以後也一定會當它是燈芯草蠟燭。」

他想證明她是否如她所說那樣，便又說：「我說那是月亮。」

「我知道那是月亮。」凱瑟琳回答。

P. 54　「妳說謊，那是神聖的太陽。」皮楚丘說。

「是神聖的太陽沒錯。」凱瑟琳回答：「如果你說它不是太陽，那它就不是太陽。你說它是什麼，它就是什麼，凱瑟琳也會認定你所說的。」

這樣，他才准她繼續上路。為了進一步測試她是否會一直這樣聽話下去，他把路上遇到的一位老先生當成小姑娘，對他說道：「早啊，高雅的姑娘。」然後問凱瑟琳是否見過比這更美的姑娘，接著他讚美老人的臉蛋又紅潤又白皙，還把他的一雙眼睛比做一對閃爍的星星。最後又對他說：「美麗的俏姑娘，祝妳日安！」然後對妻子說：「親愛的凱特，她這麼漂亮，妳給她一個擁抱吧。」

凱瑟琳如今已經完全屈服，她很快就順從丈夫的意見，也跟老先生說了同樣的話。她說：「含苞待放的小姑娘，妳長得真漂亮，又清純又甜美。妳要上哪兒？妳家住哪裡？妳父母真有福氣，生了妳這麼漂亮的孩子。」

P.55　「哎呀，凱特，你怎麼了？妳可別發瘋啊，這是個男人，一個滿臉皺紋、又乾又瘦的老男人，可不是妳說的什麼姑娘呀。」皮楚丘說。

凱瑟琳聽了答道：「老先生，請原諒我。太陽照得我眼花了，讓我把什麼都看得年輕了。現在我才看到您是個可敬的老人家，希望您原諒我這個可悲的疏忽。」

「請原諒她吧，好心的老先生。也請告訴我們您要上哪兒，如果同路，我們很樂意陪您一程。」皮楚丘說。

老紳士回答：「好先生，還有妳，這位有趣的姑娘，沒想到會這麼奇怪地碰見了你們。我叫文森修，要去找住在帕都亞的兒子。」

P.56　皮楚丘這才知道這位老人就是盧森修的父親，盧森修這位年輕人即將和巴提塔的小女兒碧安卡結婚。皮楚丘說他兒子攀上的是一門闊親事，文森修聽了很開心。他們高高興興地一起上路，來到巴提塔的家時，很多客人已經抵達，準備慶祝碧安卡和盧森修的婚禮。把凱瑟琳嫁出去之後，巴提塔就滿心歡喜地同意了碧安卡的婚事。

他們一進門，巴提塔就歡迎他們來參加婚禮，而在座的還有另外一對新婚夫婦。

　　碧安卡的丈夫盧森修和另一個剛結婚的人何天修，兩人都忍不住打趣，隱約調侃皮楚丘娶了一個潑辣的妻子。這兩個盲目自信的新郎，對於自己挑上了溫順的老婆，感到很欣慰，並嘲笑皮楚丘悲哀的選擇。

P. 57　　皮楚丘不太理會他們的玩笑，晚餐過後女士們退席，他發現連巴提塔也都加入了嘲笑他的陣容。皮楚丘堅稱她的妻子一定比他們的妻子聽話，凱瑟琳的父親聽了說道：「哎呀，皮楚丘賢婿，也真是悲哀啊，恐怕你是娶的是天字第一號的潑婦。」

P. 58　　「不見得喔！為了證明我說的是真的，我們就派人去把自己的妻子叫出來，看誰的妻子最先出來，誰的妻子就最聽話，誰也就贏得賭注。」皮楚丘說。

　　其他兩個身為人夫的男人很快同意。和頑強的凱瑟琳比起來，他們有把握自己柔順的妻子無疑是聽話多了。他們提議用二十克朗來做賭注，但皮楚丘輕鬆愉快地說道，拿獵鷹、獵犬來賭都值這麼多，自己老婆的賭注應該多個二十倍。

盧森修和何天修便將賭注加到一百克朗。盧森修先派僕人去請碧安卡過來。僕人回來時說：「先生，夫人說她正在忙，不能過來。」

「什麼？她說她正在忙，不能過來？做老婆的可以這樣回話嗎？」皮楚丘說。

P. 59　皮楚丘說罷，眾人反而嘲笑他說，只怕凱瑟琳的回覆還要更不客氣。

接著輪到何天修去叫他妻子。他跟僕人說：「去請求我妻子過來吧。」

「哦，天啊！請求她！那她一定會來囉。」皮楚丘說。

「先生呀！恐怕妳的妻子連請都請不來！」何天修說。

才說罷，這位彬彬有禮的丈夫就變了臉色，因為他看到僕人自己一個人回來，沒有帶著妻子。他問僕人說：「怎麼了，我妻子呢？」

「先生，夫人說，您大概在開什麼玩笑，所以她不過來，要您過去。」僕人說。

「愈來愈不像話了！」皮楚丘表示，他把僕人叫過來，說道：「喂，去夫人那裡，告訴她我命令她到我這裡來。」

P. 60　大家都還來不及猜她到底會不會遵命時，巴提塔就大吃一驚，叫道：「哎呀，我

SEE WHERE SHE COMES
ACT·V·SC·II·

的老天爺，凱瑟琳來了！」凱瑟琳走進門來，溫順地對皮楚丘說：「先生，你找我來有什麼吩咐嗎？」

「妳妹妹和何天修的老婆呢？」他問。

凱瑟琳回答：「她們坐在客廳的火爐邊聊天。」

「去叫她們過來吧！」皮楚丘說。

凱瑟琳沒說什麼，就依丈夫的吩咐去做。

「要說奇蹟的話，這就是奇蹟了！」盧森修說。

「的確，真不知道這是什麼預兆！」何天修說。

「哎呀，這是祥和的預兆！是恩愛、平靜生活和該當家的人當家的預兆。總之，是事事都幸福甜蜜的預兆。」皮楚丘說。

P.62　　看到女兒的改變，凱瑟琳的父親喜出望外。他說：「皮楚丘賢婿，你發了！你贏了賭注了，而且我還要再添兩萬克朗給她當嫁妝，把她當成是給另一個女兒，因為她已經完全變成另外一個人了。」

「為了讓我這賭注贏得更漂亮，我要讓你們見識一下她新學到的美德和服從。」皮楚丘說。

這時凱瑟琳帶著兩位女士走進門。他繼續說：「你們看她來了，還用婦道說服你們頑固的妻子，把她們像犯人一樣都帶來了。凱瑟琳，那頂帽子不適合妳，把那個沒用的東西拿下來，丟到腳下吧。」

凱瑟琳立刻摘下帽子，扔到地上。

「天啊！要是我哪天也做出這種傻事，我就要唉聲嘆氣了！」何天修的妻子說。

碧安卡也說：「呸，這是哪門子的愚蠢本分啊？」

P.64　碧安卡的丈夫聽了便對她說道：「我倒希望妳也能盡這種愚蠢的本分！美麗的碧安卡，從晚餐到現在，妳盡的這個本分已經使我輸了一百克朗了。」

「你更蠢，竟然拿我的本分打賭。」碧安卡說。

「凱瑟琳，我要妳去教教這些固執的女人，說說做妻子的應該對主人和丈夫盡些什麼本分。」皮楚丘說。

讓所有的人驚訝不已的是，這名改頭換面的潑婦，竟然說得頭頭是道。她讚許為人妻子的本分就是服從，就像她剛才對皮楚丘的吩咐百依百順一樣。

最後，凱瑟琳再度聞名帕都亞，但這回不再是以「潑婦凱瑟琳」而出名，而是成了帕都亞最服從盡責的妻子凱瑟琳了。

終成眷屬

P. 78　　父親剛過世，盧西昂伯爵貝特漢繼承爵位和財產。法王很喜愛貝特漢的父親，他一聽到這個死訊，就派人去召他兒子立刻前來巴黎王宮。念在和已故伯爵的一場交情上，法王打算特別照顧、拉拔年輕的貝特漢。

　　法國宮廷的老臣拉福要來帶貝特漢去見國王時，貝特漢和寡母伯爵夫人住在一起。法王是個專制的君主，他利用下諭旨或下令的方式請人去宮裡，無論多顯貴的臣民，也無法抗旨。因此，剛喪夫的伯爵夫人要和心愛的兒子分離，儘管宛如再度痛失丈夫，她仍不敢多留兒子一天，立刻囑咐他上路。

P. 79　　伯爵夫人死了丈夫，兒子又突然要離開，前來接兒子的拉福試圖安慰她。他用朝臣的那種客氣態度說，國王是個仁厚君主，會待她宛若夫君，待她兒子宛若人父。這意思是說，好心的國王會提攜貝特漢。

　　拉福還告訴伯爵夫人，國王染了重病，御醫已經宣告無藥可救。聽到國王的病

況，夫人表示十分難過。她說，但願海倫娜（在場服侍她的一位小姑娘）的父親還在人世，因為她相信海倫娜的父親一定能夠治好國王陛下的病。

P. 80 　　她跟拉福提了一下海倫娜的身世。她說，海倫娜是名醫賈合・德・枘柏的獨生女，他臨死前把女兒託付給她照顧，因此自從他死了之後，她就一直帶著海倫娜。伯爵夫人接著稱讚海倫娜本性賢慧，品德高尚，說她這些美德都承自了她那可敬的父親。

　　當她說這些話時，海倫娜不發一聲，逕自傷心地哭了起來。伯爵夫人見狀，便溫和地數落她不該為父親的死太過悲傷。

　　貝特漢向母親道別。伯爵夫人含淚辭別，一再祝福寶貝兒子，並把他託付給拉福。她說道：「我的好大人，您要多指點他，他還是個不諳世事的臣子呀。」

　　貝特漢最後跟海倫娜說了幾句話，但只是出於禮貌，祝福她快樂。臨別前，他簡短地對她說道：「善待我的母親，好好侍候妳的女主人。」

P. 82 　　海倫娜心儀貝特漢已久，事實上當她不發一聲地傷心哭泣時，那淚水並不是為了賈合・德・枘柏而流的。她愛父親，但此時此刻，她對貝特漢的情意更深，卻眼見即將要失去他。她

已經忘記死去父親的樣子和容貌，現在除了貝特漢，她心裡頭什麼人的影子也沒有。

雖然她老早就愛上了貝特漢，但她不曾忘記他是盧西昂伯爵，是法國最古老家族的後裔，而她卻出身低微，父母名不見經傳。貝特漢的祖先都是貴族，所以她把出身高貴的貝特漢當作是主人，是她親愛的少爺。除了終身服侍他，做一輩子的家僕，她不敢有任何奢望。

他地位尊貴，她出身低下，兩人身世懸殊。她常說：「我愛上一顆閃耀明星，還想和星星結婚。貝特漢太高不可攀了。」

P. 84 貝特漢離開了。她淚眼婆娑，傷心不已。她愛他，但不認為兩人有希望，而能夠時時刻刻看到他，她已經心滿意足了。她會坐下來，仰望他的深色眼眸、彎彎眉毛和柔軟的鬢髮，直到彷彿能在心版上畫出他的肖像。那心愛臉龐上的每一個線條，她都牢記在心裡。

賈合‧德‧柄柏過世後沒有留下遺產，只留了一些珍貴良方給她。那些都是他在醫學上深入研究和長期試驗所獲得的，幾乎是萬無一失的藥方。

拉福說，國王害了病，日漸虛弱，而其中正好有個處方寫明可以醫治。一聽說國王龍體不適，海倫娜雖仍不免覺得自己出身卑微，希望渺茫，但心下還是起了個雄心計畫，打算隻身前往巴黎，救治國王。

P. 85 海倫娜手裡是握有這籤祕方，但國王和御醫既然已認定無藥可救，因此即使她請求醫治，諒他們也不見得會相信一個無學無知的姑娘。但她堅信，只要獲准一試，成功的把握可能還會比父親醫術所能保證的來得更大，即使父親生前是最聞名的大夫。她感受到一股強大的信念，覺得這帖良藥蒙受天上一切

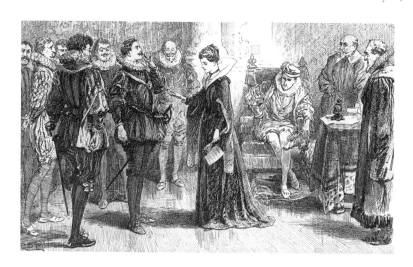

吉星之眷顧，是一份足以改善她命運的遺產，甚至可以使她高攀成為盧西昂伯爵夫人。

貝特漢離開不久，管家就通報伯爵夫人說，他無意中聽到海倫娜在自言自語，從她的隻字片語中，知道她愛上了貝特漢，想跟他到巴黎去。伯爵夫人謝過管家，要他下去，並通知海倫娜過來，她有話要跟她說。

聽到海倫娜的事，伯爵夫人不禁往事湧上心頭。那時，約莫是她剛愛上貝特漢的父親之際，她自言自語說：「我年輕時也是這個樣子的。愛情，是青春玫瑰上的一根刺。我們是自然之子，青春時代時不免犯了這些錯，儘管當時並不以為有錯。」

伯爵夫人正沉思自己青春時代所犯的愛情過錯時，海倫娜走了進來。

夫人對她說：「海倫娜，妳知道我就像是妳的母親。」

海倫娜回答：「您是我尊貴的女主人。」

伯爵夫人再度強調：「妳是我的女兒，為什麼一聽我說我是妳的母親，妳就臉色蒼白？」

海倫娜擔心夫人瞧出她的心思，所以一臉驚惶，思緒慌亂。她依舊回答：「夫人，請原諒我，您並不是我的母親，盧西昂伯爵不可能是我哥哥，我也不是您的女兒。」

P. 88　　伯爵夫人說：「可是海倫娜，妳可以做我的兒媳婦。我想妳是有此意，所以『母親』和『女兒』這兩個詞才讓妳不安。海倫娜，妳愛不愛我兒子？」

「好心的夫人，您原諒我啊。」驚慌的海倫娜說道。

伯爵夫人又問了一次同樣的問題：「妳愛不愛我兒子嗎？」

「您不也愛他嗎，夫人？」海倫娜說。

伯爵夫人回答：「海倫娜，妳答話不要閃爍其詞。來吧，把妳的心意講出來，大家都看得出來妳的愛意了。」

海倫娜跪了下來，坦承自己的感情，又羞又驚地乞求這個貴族女主人原諒她。她表示自己知道兩人門不當戶不對，並表示貝特漢不知道她的情意。她把她卑微無望的愛比喻成一個可憐的印地安人：印地安人崇拜太陽，太陽雖然也照耀著這位崇拜者，可是卻不知道他究竟是何人。

P. 89　　伯爵夫人問海倫娜最近是否想去巴黎。她坦承，當她聽到拉福提到國王的病時，心裡的確起了這個念頭。

「這是妳想去巴黎的動機嗎？」伯爵夫人說：「是嗎？妳老實說。」

海倫娜老實答道：「是少爺讓我起了這個念頭，要不然，什麼巴黎、藥方或國王，我當時都不會想到。」

聽了這番完整的告白，伯爵夫人沒說半句贊成或是責怪的話，只是認真盤問海倫娜那帖藥方是否真有可能救治國王。

P. 90　伯爵夫人發現，那是賈合・德・柯柏所有藥方中最珍貴的一箋，他在臨終前才傳給女兒。她又想起那可怕的一刻，她正式答應過要照顧這姑娘。如今，這位姑娘的命運和國王的性命，似乎都要看這計畫能否實現了（計畫雖是出自一位痴情姑娘的痴心想法，但伯爵夫人心想那或許是天意，冥冥之中要醫治好國王，也讓賈合・德・柯柏之女的未來命運有個好基礎）。於是她准許海倫娜完全按自己的意思進行，又慷慨資助她充分的盤纏，並派了幾個妥當的隨從跟去。帶著伯爵夫人的祝福，以及盼望她成功的好心祈願，海倫娜隨即往巴黎而去。

P. 91　海倫娜抵達巴黎後，靠著老臣子拉福這位友人的幫忙，她獲准晉見國王。但是她還得面臨許多難關，因為要勸國王試服這位美麗年輕大夫所獻的藥方，並非易事。她告訴國王，自己是賈合・德・柯柏的女兒（國王早就聞其大名），而她所獻的珍貴藥方，宛如珍寶，集父親長年經驗和醫術之精華。她還大膽承諾，如果兩天之內，不能使陛下完全恢復健康，那她甘受死罪。

P. 93　國王最後答應一試。兩天之內，國王若無法病癒，海倫娜就得受死；然而要是她成功了，國王答應任由她在全法國的男子之中（除了王子之外），挑選中意的人為夫。要是她能治好國王的病，她所要求的報酬就是任她挑選自己的丈夫。

海倫娜料想得沒錯，父親的藥方果然奏效，沒讓她希望落空。不出兩天，國王就完全恢復了健康。他召集宮中所有年輕的貴族，以便依約報償，賜給美麗大夫一位新郎。他要海倫娜瞧瞧這群年輕的單身貴族，挑一個來做丈夫。

海倫娜很快做好選擇，因為她在這群年輕的臣子當中瞥見了盧西昂伯爵。她轉向貝特漢，說道：「就是這一位了。少爺，我不敢說我挑中了您，但只要我在世，蒙您指導，我就把自己獻給您，為您服務。」

King. Now, fair one, does your business follow us?
Helena. Ay, my good lord.

Act II. Scene I.

P.94 國王說：「啊，那麼，年輕的貝特漢，把她帶回去吧，她是你的妻子了。」

貝特漢毫不遲疑地公然表示：他不喜歡國王的這個賞賜。他說，這個自己送上門的海倫娜是個窮大夫的女兒，她從前在她父親的照料下長大，現在則靠他母親的施惠過活。

聽到他說這些拒絕的輕蔑話，海倫娜對國王說：「陛下，見您康復，我就很高興了，其他的就作罷吧。」

但國王容不得他的諭旨被藐視，賜與貴族婚姻可是法王的眾多特權之一。於是，貝特漢只好當天娶進海倫娜。對貝特漢而言，這是一樁不稱心的逼婚，對那位可憐的姑娘來說，也沒

有遠景可言。她冒著生命的
危險，得到這個貴族丈夫，
可是贏來的似乎只是一場空
歡喜，因為丈夫的心並不是
法王權力所能賜與的禮物。

P.96　　一結完婚，貝特漢就要
海倫娜代他向國王請求，答
應讓他離開宮廷。當她告知
國王已批准他離開時，貝特
漢告訴她，對於這場突如其
來的婚姻，他毫無準備，十
分苦惱，因此對於他下一步
的打算，她也不需要感到驚
訝。

King. Know'st thou not, Bertram,
What she has done for me?
Bertram.　　Yes, my good lord;
But never hope to know why I should marry her.
Act II. Scene III.

　　就算她不驚訝，但發現他有意要離開她，她也不免傷心。

　　他命令她回到他母親的家。聽到他這無情的話，海倫娜說
道：「先生，這件事我無話可說。我的出身不起眼，不配享有
這種福氣，但我是你最順從的僕人，絕對會真心侍奉您，好彌
補這種缺憾。」

　　然而海倫娜這番謙卑的說辭，絲毫也不能打動高傲的貝特
漢，讓他憐惜這溫柔的妻子。他甚至連道別時的親切客套話也
沒說，就離開了她。

P.98　　海倫娜只好回到伯爵夫人的身邊。她完成了這趟旅程的目
的，既救了國王一命，也和心愛的少爺盧西昂伯爵成了親。然
而當她沮喪地回到貴族婆婆那裡時，才一進家門，就收到貝特
漢的一封信，幾乎教她斷腸。

好心的伯爵夫人熱忱接待她，當她是兒子親自挑選的妻子，視她是出身高貴的婦人。看到貝特漢惡意冷落，新婚之日就打發她一人獨自回家，伯爵夫人說了一些好話來安慰她。

但親切的接待並不能排解海倫娜心裡的悲傷。她說：「夫人，我丈夫走了，永遠不會回來了。」

她讀著貝特漢的信：

等妳拿到我手上這枚永遠也不會拿下來的戒指時，
再叫我丈夫吧，但是「永遠」都不會有「那一刻」的。

P. 99 「這真是可怕的宣判！」海倫娜說。

伯爵夫人請她耐下性子，說貝特漢現在是走了，但她就是她的孩子了，理當是個貴族，受得起讓二十個像貝特漢這種粗魯男孩來服侍她，終日稱她為夫人。可是無論這位仁厚無比的婆婆如何屈尊地尊重她，如何好心地討好她，都無法撫慰兒媳婦的悲傷。

海倫娜的眼睛直盯著信看，傷心欲絕地哭喊道：

妻子一日尚在，
法國就無一日值得我留戀的地方。

伯爵夫人問她：這句話是否是信裡所寫的？

「正是，夫人。」可憐的海倫娜只能這樣回答。

P. 100　　第二天早上，海倫娜失蹤了。她走後留下一封信給伯爵夫人，向她說明自己突然離去的緣由。她在信裡說道，她逼得貝特漢離開故鄉家園，心中萬分難過。為了彌補過失，她要前往聖佳克‧勒‧葛洪聖壇朝聖。最後，她請伯爵夫人通知她兒子，說他痛恨的妻子已經永遠離開他的家園了。

　　離開巴黎後，貝特漢來到佛羅倫斯，在佛羅倫斯公爵的軍隊裡頭當軍官。一場勝役後，他因作戰驍勇，顯赫一時。之後他收到母親的來信，得知海倫娜不再糾纏他的好消息。

　　就在他準備啟程返家時，穿著朝聖裝的海倫娜也來到了佛羅倫斯城。

P. 102　　在以前，佛羅倫斯是朝聖者前往聖佳克‧勒‧葛洪的必經城市。海倫娜來到這個城市之後，聽說當地有一個殷勤好客的寡婦，時常在家裡接待前往那位聖徒神廟的女朝聖者，除了親切款待，並供給住宿。海倫娜跑去找這位善心女士，寡婦殷勤招呼她，邀請她去參觀這座名城的各種新奇事物，還問她是否想瞧瞧公爵的軍隊，她可以帶她到能夠一覽整個軍旅的地方。

「而且妳還會看到貴國的同胞。」寡婦說：「他叫盧西昂伯爵，在公爵的戰役中建功立勳。」

一聽到能夠看到貝特漢，海倫娜不需寡婦再三邀請，就答應前去。她隨女東道主一道走，想到能夠再見到親愛丈夫的臉，那種喜悅真是既傷心又悲涼。

「這男人長得很俊秀吧？」寡婦說。

「我很喜歡他。」海倫娜由衷地回答。

P. 104 她們沿途走著，健談的寡婦一路上談的都是貝特漢。她把貝特漢的婚姻經過告訴海倫娜，說他如何遺棄那個嫁給他的可憐婦人，為了不和她住在一起，還跑來加入公爵的軍隊。

海倫娜耐心聽著自己不幸的遭遇，但說完了這些，貝特漢的故事卻還沒結束。寡婦接下來又講起另一個故事。這故事的字字句句都刺痛海倫娜的心，因為寡婦說的是貝特漢如何迷戀她女兒。

貝特漢是不喜歡國王逼他成親，但他看起來也不是個不懂愛情的人。他隨軍隊駐紮佛羅倫斯時，愛上了年輕貌美的淑女黛安娜，也就是這位接待海倫娜的寡婦之女。每晚，他都會來黛安娜的窗下追求她，彈奏各種音樂，高唱歌曲，歌頌她的美貌。他所請求的，無非不是要黛安娜允許他在她家人都歇息之

後，偷偷去和她相會。

P. 106　可是黛安娜知道他是已婚男子，所以無論如何也不為所動，既不肯答應這個不成體統的要求，也不回應他的追求。黛安娜是在嚴母的教導下長大的，雖然寡婦現在家道中落，但也是系出名門，為開普雷世家的後代。

　　好心的夫人把這些都告訴了海倫娜，她大大誇獎她這謹慎的女兒恪守禮教，又說這完全要歸功於她給她的良好教育和教誨。她又說，貝特漢最近特別糾纏不清，期待黛安娜今晚首肯一見，因為他隔天一早就要離開佛羅倫斯了。

　　聽到貝特漢愛上寡婦的女兒，海倫娜很難過。但又聽她這麼一說，海倫娜急中生智，計畫找回逃婚的丈夫。（雖然上次的計畫失敗，但她並不氣餒）

　　她向寡婦表白自己就是貝特漢的棄婦海倫娜。她請求好心的女東道主和她的女兒這次能接受貝特漢的來訪，並允許她代替黛安娜和貝特漢相會。她告訴她們，她這次想和丈夫偷偷相會，主要是為了拿到他的戒指。丈夫曾說過，只要她拿到那枚戒指，他就承認她是他的妻子。

P. 107　寡婦和她的女兒很同情這個不幸的棄婦，再加上海倫娜答應酬謝她們，讓她們很心動，便答應相助此事。海倫娜先給她們一袋錢，作為日後酬謝的定金。

當天，海倫娜要人送消息給貝特漢，說她已經去世。希望他聽到她的死訊後，認為自己有權可以再物色他人，然後向假扮黛安娜的海倫娜求婚。只要能夠得到戒指和結婚諾言，她相信自己就能讓這件事有好的結果。

P. 108　　傍晚天黑之後，貝特漢獲准進入黛安娜的繡房，而海倫娜早就在裡頭準備好接待他了。

　　他對海倫娜傾吐纏綿情話，儘管她心裡明白這些話是說給黛安娜聽的，但仍覺得珍貴。貝特漢非常迷戀她，鄭重承諾要做他的丈夫，永遠愛她。海倫娜希望，要是有一天，他知道了這個跟自己相談甚歡的人，竟是自己所鄙視的妻子時，這些諾言到時候可以變成真實的愛情。

　　貝特漢從來沒發現過海倫娜是個聰明的姑娘，要不然，他可能就不會那樣看不上她了。再加上兩人天天相見，他也就完全沒注意到她的美麗。要是習慣常常見到某人的臉孔，就無法像第一眼見到時那樣，留下深刻的美醜印象。另外，貝特漢也無法感受到海倫娜的善解人意，她對他如此敬愛，所以她在他面前時總是不發一語。

P. 110　　可現在，她日後的命運和她的愛情計畫是否皆能圓滿落幕，都得看她今晚相會時能否在貝特漢的心中留下美好印象，於是她竭盡所能來討他歡心。她言談活潑，坦率又通情達理，態度可愛又甜美，讓貝特漢傾心不已，貝特漢於是宣誓娶她為妻。

海倫娜要他脫下戒指，做為定情之物，他於是交上戒指。對她來說，擁有這枚戒指很重要，而她則把國王御賜的戒指拿給他，以做為交換。

早晨天色未明之際，她送走貝特漢，貝特漢立刻啟程返回母親家。

海倫娜說服寡婦和黛安娜跟她一道回巴黎。為完全實現她的計畫，她需要她們進一步的支援。她們抵達巴黎時，發現國王已去拜訪盧西昂伯爵夫人，海倫娜於是盡全力欲趕上國王。

P. 111　國王龍體已經大安，但仍滿心感激海倫娜救了他。他一見到盧西昂伯爵夫人，就聊起海倫娜，說海倫娜是她兒子因為愚蠢而失去的一顆珍貴寶石。伯爵夫人為海倫娜的死正傷慟不已，國王看到自己的話又讓她傷心，只好說道：「我的好夫人，這一切我都已經原諒了，也已經忘了。」

本性善良的老拉福也在場，他無法忍受他心疼的海倫娜這樣被人輕易遺忘。他說：「這下子臣非說不可了，這個年輕的臣子對他的國王陛下、母親

和妻子，都太不知分寸了。不過他最對不起的還是他自己，因為他失去了一個令人驚艷的美麗妻子，而且她說話讓人信服，十全十美，任誰都想服侍她。」

P. 113　　國王表示：「讚美逝者，愈添美好回憶。這樣吧，把他叫過來。」國王指的是貝特漢，現在他人就在國王面前。他對自己傷害海倫娜的事，深表歉意。看在他的亡父和可敬母親的份上，國王饒恕了他，恢復對他的寵幸。

　　未料，國王的慈顏卻突然對他愀然變色，原來，國王看到他手上戴著自己御賜給海倫娜的戒指。國王記得一清二楚，海倫娜曾對著所有聖徒立誓，永遠不讓戒指離手，當她遭遇重大變故時，才會把戒指送還給國王本人。國王追問他戒指是哪兒來的，貝特漢編了一個離奇的謊言，說是一位姑娘從窗台上丟給他的，並且表示他從結婚那天以後，就沒再見過海倫娜。

　　國王知道貝特漢不中意妻子，擔心他把她殺害，便下令侍衛捉拿貝特漢，說道：「我腦裡縈繞著一種可怕的想法，我怕海倫娜已經慘遭謀殺了。」

P. 114　　這時，黛安娜和母親走進來向國王請願，請求陛下運用王權強迫貝特漢娶黛安娜，因為他對她有過正式的婚約宣誓。貝特漢怕國王生氣，連忙否認自己宣誓過。黛安娜於是取出戒指（海倫娜把它交到她手裡的），證實自己所言不假。她表示，他發誓娶她時，為了還禮，就把貝特漢現在所戴著的戒指送給他。

　　一聽到這裡，國王命令侍衛也將她拿下。她和貝特漢兩人對戒指的說辭不一樣，更加確認國王所疑有據。國王表示，要是他們不招供海倫娜的戒指從何得來，兩人就要一併處斬。

　　黛安娜請求讓她母親去把那個賣戒指給她的珠寶商帶來，國王批准。寡婦離開不久，就帶著海倫娜本人回來。

看到兒子處境危險，好伯爵夫人默默地兀自傷悲，也很害怕兒子殺妻的嫌疑會是真的。如今看到她曾視如己出的親愛的海倫娜還活著，她欣喜欲狂。國王同樣也喜出望外，不敢相信那人就是海倫娜，他說：「我看到的這個人真的就是貝特漢的妻子嗎？」

P. 116　　海倫娜自覺妻子的身分尚未獲得承認，就答道：「不，好陛下，您看到的只是一個妻子的影子罷了，有名無實。」

貝特漢大喊：「有名有實！有名有實！啊，原諒我吧！」

海倫娜表示：「喔，少爺，我扮成這位美麗姑娘時，發現你非常體貼。你看，這是你寫的信！」她用愉快的語調，把她一度傷心反覆唸過的話讀給他聽：等妳拿到我手上這只永遠也

不會拿下來的戒指時……「我辦到了，你把戒指給了我。如今我贏得你兩次了，你願意做我的丈夫嗎？」

P. 117　　貝特漢回答：「只要妳能證明那天晚上和我談話的女子就是妳，那我就會永遠好好地愛妳。」

　　這並不難，因為寡婦和黛安娜隨海倫娜一道來，正是為了證明這件事實。海倫娜效勞過國王，國王很看重她，又因黛安娜好心幫助海倫娜，於是國王也很喜歡黛安娜。為此，國王也許了黛安娜一位貴族丈夫。海倫娜的事給了國王一個啟示：美麗姑娘要是有了特別的功勞，國王最佳的賞賜就是賜給她們丈夫。

　　就這樣，海倫娜終於知道，父親留下的遺產果然蒙受天上一切吉星之眷顧。如今，她是親愛的貝特漢所鍾愛的妻子，是貴族夫人的兒媳婦，而她自己也貴為盧西昂伯爵夫人了。

一報還一報

P. 132　　一位性情溫和寬宏的公爵曾經治理過維也納城，他對人民從不採用嚴刑峻法。特別是有一條法律，因公爵在位期間還未曾執行過，所以幾乎被人遺忘。

　　這條法律規定，凡與妻子以外的婦女同居，一律處死。因公爵寬大，這條法律完全受到漠視，神聖的婚姻制度不被重視，天天可見有年輕女兒的維也納父母跑來見公爵，投訴他們照顧的女兒被勾引，跑去和單身男子同居。

P. 133　　看到民間這種不良風氣愈來愈熾盛，好心的公爵很難過。但他想，自己向來為政寬厚，若為了匡正惡習，突然變得嚴律苛政，（一向擁戴他的）人民必定會把他當成暴君。

　　為此，他決定暫時離開公國，由代理人全權掌政。如此一來，既可執法禁止不當的戀愛行為，自己也不用因為變得嚴苛而招致民怨。

　　公爵選了安哲羅來擔當此項重責大任。安哲羅是個因生活嚴謹而在維也納享有聖徒之譽的人，公爵認為他是最佳人選。公爵跟御前參事艾斯卡大臣透露此計，艾斯卡表示：「在維也納城，能配享此隆恩光榮者，就屬安哲羅大人了。」

P. 135 公爵托詞要去波蘭。在他離開維也納的告假期間，由安哲羅擔任攝政。事實上，公爵出城只是個幌子，他悄悄返回維也納，喬裝成修士，打算暗中觀察這看似聖人的安哲羅的作為。

就在安哲羅受命就任新職後不久，有位叫做克勞狄的紳士，將一位年輕姑娘從她父母身邊誘拐走。對於這宗罪行，新任攝政下令，將克勞狄收押並打入牢裡。安哲羅根據這條被忽視已久的舊有法律，判克勞狄斬首處決。

請求寬恕年輕克勞狄的聲浪高漲，連好心的老臣艾斯卡本人也為他說項：「哎呀，我想搭救的這位先生有個德高望重的父親，看在他父親的份上，請求您寬恕這年輕人的罪。」

P. 136 安哲羅回答：「法律不能像稻草人一樣，豎立起來只為嚇唬來捕食的鳥。鳥習慣之後，見稻草人傷不了自己，不但不再怕它，還會在上頭棲息。大人，他非死不可。」

好友陸西歐去監獄探視克勞狄。克勞狄對他說：「拜託你，陸西歐，幫我個忙，去找我姐姐伊莎貝拉，她今天就要進聖克雷修道院了。請告訴她我情況危急，求她去和嚴苛的攝政說說情，親自去見安哲羅一趟。她辯才無礙，善於勸說，而且她少女的憂鬱中有某種難喻的特質，足以打動男人，我想這樣成功的希望會很大。」

正如克勞狄所說，姐姐伊莎貝拉當天進入修道院見習，準備在通過修女的見習期後，正式成為修女。正當她向一位修女詢問修道院的清規時，她們聽到了陸西歐的聲音。陸西歐走進修道院，說道：「願主賜與此地平安！」

「是誰在說話？」伊莎貝拉說。

「是男人的聲音。」修女答道:「好伊莎貝拉,妳去看看,問他有何貴事。妳可以去,我不行。成為修女之後,除了當著修道院長的面之外,不可以和任何異性說話,而且說話時也不能露出自己的臉,如果露出臉,就不可以說話。」

「妳們修女還有其他權利嗎?」伊莎貝拉問。

「這些還不夠嗎?」修女回答。

「不,夠了。」伊莎貝拉說:「我這麼問並不是想要更多的權利,而是希望侍奉聖克雷的姊妹們能持更嚴格的清規。」

她們又聽到陸西歐的聲音。修女說:「他又在叫了,請妳去招呼他吧。」

伊莎貝拉走出去見陸西歐,向他回禮致意,說道:「平安豐足!是誰在說話?」

陸西歐恭敬地走向她,說道:「這位童貞女,天佑妳。妳臉頰紅潤,應當就是一位童貞女吧!能請妳帶我去見伊莎貝拉嗎?她是這裡的見習修女,也是一位不幸兄弟克勞狄的美麗姐姐。」

「請問,為什麼說是不幸的兄弟?」伊莎貝拉說:「我就是他的姐姐伊莎貝拉。」

「美麗溫柔的小姐。」他回答：「妳弟弟要我好好問候妳，他坐牢了。」

「哎呀！怎麼一回事啊？」伊莎貝拉問。

陸西歐告訴她，克勞狄因為勾引一位少女，身陷囹圄。

她說：「噯，該不會是表妹茱麗葉吧。」

茱麗葉和伊莎貝拉並非親戚，但為紀念兩人在學校時的情誼，便互稱表姊妹。伊莎貝

拉知道茱麗葉迷戀克勞狄，擔心她會因愛戀他而犯錯。

「正是她。」陸西歐回答。

「那就讓我弟弟娶茱麗葉呀。」伊莎貝拉說。

陸西歐表示，克勞狄是很樂意娶茱麗葉，但因他違法，攝政將他判了死刑。他說：「這下只能靠妳了，用好話去說動安哲羅。妳不幸的弟弟要我來找妳，正為此事。」

P. 141　伊莎貝拉說：「唉！我有什麼能耐幫他？我想我沒有辦法讓安哲羅改變心意的。」

「疑惑足以敗事呀。」陸西歐說：「害怕嘗試，讓我們錯失可能成功的機會。去找安哲羅大人吧！姑娘們只要跪下來求情，哭訴一番，男人就會像上帝一樣慷慨大方了。」

「我試試看好了。」伊莎貝拉說：「我先留下來跟院長報告這件事，然後再去找安哲羅。代我轉告我弟弟，能不能成功，我今晚就會給他消息。」

伊莎貝拉趕去宮廷，跪在安哲羅的面前說：「大人啊，我是個苦命人，請大人聽我申訴呀。」

「妳有什麼要申訴的？」安哲羅問。

她於是用最動人的話，乞求讓弟弟免於一死。

P. 143　安哲羅說：「姑娘啊，這件事情已經沒有挽回的餘地，令弟已經定罪，是非死不可了。」

「啊，律法公正，只是太苛！」伊莎貝拉說：「這麼說來，到時候我也沒了弟弟。上帝祝福您！」說罷就準備離開。

陪她前來的陸西歐說道：「別輕言放棄啊。再回去哀求他，跪在他面前，抓住他的袍子。妳的態度太冷淡了，就算是討一根針，也得說得懇切一些才行啊。」

於是伊莎貝拉再度下跪請求開恩。

安哲羅說：「已經定罪了，太遲了。」

「太遲！」伊莎貝拉說：「不，不遲！說出口的話可以收回。大人，請您相信，大人物的任何儀仗，舉凡是國王的皇冠、攝政的寶劍、元帥的權杖，或是法官的長袍，比起仁慈所能彰顯的偉大，都還不及一半。」

P. 144　「請妳走吧。」安哲羅說。

但伊莎貝拉仍向他懇求道：「如果把我弟弟換作是您，把您換作是他，您也可能犯同樣的錯，可是他就不會像您這樣嚴厲。但願我有您的權力，而您變成是伊莎貝拉，那我會這樣對

待您嗎？不會的。我要讓您了解做法官的滋味，也要讓您了解做犯人又是什麼滋味。」

「夠了，好姑娘！」安哲羅說：「定妳弟弟罪的是法律，不是我。就算他是我的親戚、手足或兒子，法律還是會這樣定他的罪，他明天非死不可了。」

「明天？」伊莎貝拉說：「啊！這太突然了，饒了他，饒了他吧，他還沒有準備好就死。我們就是在廚房裡宰殺雞鴨，也有個季節時令，對獻給上天的東西，難道比對餵飽我們這賤命的食物還草率嗎？好心的大人呀，您想想，犯此罪者何其多，就從未有人因為做我弟弟所做之事而斷送性命。您是第一個定這種罪的人，他是第一個遭受這種刑罰的人。大人啊，請您摸著良心，捫心自問知不知道我弟弟犯的是什麼罪，要是您的良心承認自己也有犯這種罪的本能，那就不要有判我弟弟死罪的想法！」

P. 145　　她最後所說的這些話，比之前所說的更加動搖了安哲羅，因為伊莎貝拉的美貌讓他心裡起了邪念。就像克勞狄所犯的罪

270

一樣，他開始有了不正當愛情的念頭。這些內心的衝突使他別過臉，轉身離開伊莎貝拉。伊莎貝拉把他叫回來，說道：「仁慈的大人啊，請您回過身來，聽聽我怎麼賄賂你，好心的大人啊，請轉過身來吧！」

「什麼，賄賂我！」安哲羅說。他很訝異她竟想賄賂他。

P. 146　　「對啊。」伊莎貝拉說：「用連上帝也會與你分享的禮物賄賂你。不是用金銀財寶，也不是用全憑人類喜好而決定價值的閃亮寶石，而是用在日出之前就能傳達到天堂的虔誠祈禱──由無瑕的靈魂、全心奉獻給上帝的齋戒女子所祈禱的。」

「好吧，妳明天再來找我。」安哲羅說。

弟弟暫時得到緩刑，伊莎貝拉獲准再度上訴，她離開攝政時滿懷喜悅，希望最後能夠改變攝政嚴苛的個性。她臨走時，說道：「願上帝保佑大人平安！願上帝拯救大人！」安哲羅聽到，就在心裡說道：「阿門！願上帝保佑我不要被妳和妳的美德所惑。」

緊接著，他被自己的這些邪念嚇到，說道：「怎麼回事？怎麼回事？我愛上她了嗎？竟想再聽到她說話，想再盯著她的眼睛看？我在痴想什麼呀？人類那狡獪的敵人為了讓聖徒上鉤，就用聖徒來當釣餌。我從沒對放蕩的婦人動心過，可是這個貞潔的女子卻把我治得服服

貼貼。即使是現在，男子痴戀女子時，我都還笑他們，覺得他們莫名其妙。」

P. 147 　　當天晚上，安哲羅內心掙扎，充滿罪惡感，比那個被他判了死刑的犯人還難受，因為穿著修士服的好公爵去了牢裡探視克勞狄。公爵指點這個年輕人通往天堂的路，告訴他如何懺悔和祈求平安。

　　要不要做壞事，安哲羅搖擺不定，甚感痛苦。他一下子想誘惑伊莎貝拉遠離清白貞潔的修道，一下子又為自己的犯罪念頭感到悔恨惶恐。最後，壞念頭佔了上風。這個之前還為賄賂行為大吃一驚的人，如今決定對這位少女大大行賄一番，甚至可以用她親愛弟弟的性命來當做珍貴的賄禮，讓她拒絕不了。

　　早上，伊莎貝拉前來，安哲羅要她單獨進來見他。進來之後，他對她說，如果她願意把她的初夜獻給他，和他做茱麗葉與克勞狄違法所做的事情，那他就可以饒她弟弟一命。

P. 149 　　他說：「因為，伊莎貝拉，我愛妳。」

　　伊莎貝拉說：「我弟弟也愛茱麗葉，你說他要為此送上性命。」

　　安哲羅說：「克勞狄不該死了，只要你答應晚上偷偷跑來找我，就像茱麗葉半夜蹺家去找克勞狄一樣。」

　　他的話讓伊莎貝拉很吃驚，他定她弟弟的罪，卻又引誘她去犯相同的罪。她說：「為了我不幸的弟弟，也為了我自己，也就是說，若我被判了死刑，我會把身上的一條條鞭痕，當作是穿戴了紅色寶石，像走向我渴望躺上去的床一樣地走向死亡，也不會讓自己蒙受這種恥辱。」她還說，但願他說這些話只是為了考驗她的貞節。

　　他說：「相信我，我以人格擔保，我所說的都是我的本意。」

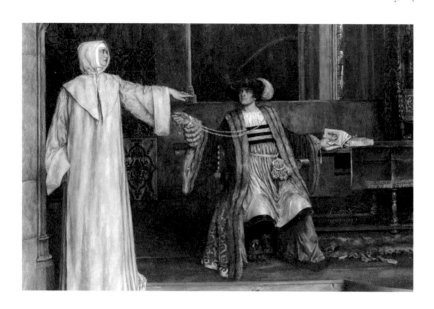

P. 150　　　聽到他用「人格」這兩個字來表示這麼齷齪的念頭，伊莎貝拉很惱怒，說道：「哈！你這麼居心不良，有多少人格可以相信呀！安哲羅，我要舉發你，你等著吧！你要不現在就簽一張赦免我弟弟的命令，要不我就到處大聲張揚你是一個什麼樣的人！」

　　　「伊莎貝拉，誰會相信妳？」安哲羅說：「我名聲毫無污點，生活一絲不苟，我那反駁妳的話，遠比妳那控訴我的話更有分量。好好為令弟著想，答應我的要求吧，不然他明天就得死了。至於妳，隨妳怎麼說吧，我的謊言是比妳的實話更有分量的。妳明天就給我答案吧。」

P. 151　　　「我該向誰喊冤啊？就算我說了，又有誰會相信我？」伊莎貝拉說著，一面走向弟弟被囚禁的陰暗地牢。她到地牢時，弟弟正和公爵談論著神。穿著修士服的公爵也探訪過茱麗葉，讓這對犯罪的戀人清楚自己所犯的過錯。痛苦的茱麗葉流著淚，真心懺悔，告白自己比克勞狄更應該受到責罰，因為是自己心甘情願同意了他那不正當的請求。

伊莎貝拉走進克勞狄被囚禁的牢房，一面說：「願主賜與此地平安、恩典和良伴！」

「是誰？」喬裝過的公爵說：「進來吧，這種祝福受人歡迎。」

「我來跟克勞狄說一兩句話。」伊莎貝拉說。

P. 152 公爵留下他們兩人，要看守犯人的獄吏帶他到一個可以偷聽到他們講話的地方。

「姐姐，現在有什麼好消息嗎？」克勞狄問。

伊莎貝拉告訴他得準備明天受死。

「沒有挽救的餘地了嗎？」克勞狄問。

「有啊，弟弟。」伊莎貝拉回答：「是有一個，不過要是你同意了，那你就會名譽掃地，無臉見人。」

「告訴我怎麼回事。」克勞狄說。

「哦，克勞狄，我真替你擔心！」姐姐回答：「我很害怕你貪生，把多個短短六、七寒暑的壽命看得比一生的名譽還重要。你敢勇於面對死亡嗎？死亡大都是想像時覺得可怕，踩在我們腳下的可憐甲蟲，牠們死時和巨人死時一樣痛苦。」

P. 154　「妳為什麼要這樣羞辱我？」克勞狄說：「妳以為溫柔的慰藉可以讓我變得堅毅嗎？若我終究得死，我會把黑暗當作新娘，將它擁入懷裡。」

　　「這才像是我弟弟說的話。」伊莎貝拉說：「這才是父親墳裡傳出來的聲音。你終究得死，但是克勞狄，你想得到嗎？那個貌似聖人的攝政說，只要我把貞操獻給他，他就饒你一命。啊，如果他要的是我的命，為了救你，我會像丟一根針一樣，毫不在乎地就給他！」

　　「謝謝妳，親愛的伊莎貝拉。」克勞狄說。

　　「你該為明天的受死做準備了。」伊莎貝拉說。

　　「死亡是件很恐怖的事。」克勞狄說。

　　「但可恥的生活令人痛恨。」他的姐姐回答。

　　但此時克勞狄一想到死亡，他堅定的個性就動搖了。只有臨死的罪犯才能感受到那種恐懼的侵襲，他叫道：「好姐姐，讓我活下去！妳犯罪是為了要救弟弟一命，上天會恩准這種行為，它會成為一種美德的。」

P. 157　「哦，意志不堅的懦夫！虛偽卑鄙的小人！」伊莎貝拉說：「你要讓你姐蒙羞來苟且偷生？哦，呸，呸，呸！弟弟，我還以為你

275

是個很有榮譽感的人，以為
你要是有二十顆腦袋，寧可
上二十個斷頭台，也不願讓
自己的姐姐受這種屈辱。」

「不，伊莎貝拉，妳聽
我說！」克勞狄說。

他想為自己辯解，解
釋自己為何軟弱到要靠貞潔
的姐姐屈節來苟活，但公爵
走了進來，打斷他的話。他
說：「克勞狄，你和你姐姐
說的話我都聽到了。安哲羅
絕對無意染指她，他說那些

話不過是想考驗她的品德。她真的是個貞潔女子，得體地拒絕
了他，他高興都來不及了。他是不可能赦免你的，你就趁剩下
的一點時間來祈禱，為死亡做好準備吧。」

P. 158　　克勞狄後悔自己剛剛的懦弱，他說：「讓我求我姐原諒我
吧！我不再眷戀生命，但求一死。」克勞狄說完就退到一旁，
為自己的過錯愧疚懊悔不已。

這時公爵單獨和伊莎貝拉在一起。他稱讚她守貞不渝，說
道：「上帝賦與妳美貌，也賦與妳美德。」

伊莎貝拉說：「唉，安哲羅竟這樣蒙蔽了好心的公爵！等
公爵回來，若我能見到他的話，一定要揭發他的治理情況。」
伊莎貝拉不知道她已經在揭發她揚言要揭發的事情了。

公爵回答：「那樣做並無不妥，但就目前的情況看來，安
哲羅一定會駁倒妳的控訴的，因此妳不妨聽聽我的忠告。有個

276

不幸女子被冤枉，我想妳可以仗義幫助她，而且還可以讓妳弟弟免受峻法。妳不但不需要讓自己的貞潔之身受到玷污，而且要是外出的公爵回來，知道了這件事，也會非常高興的。」

P. 160　　伊莎貝拉表示，只要不是壞事，他要她做什麼都行。

　　「有德者勇，無所畏懼。」公爵說。他接著問她，是否聽過瑪莉安娜這個人，她是在海上溺斃的偉大軍人弗烈德的妹妹。

　　「我聽過這位淑女。」伊莎貝拉說：「一說到她，聽到的都是好話。」

　　公爵說：「她是安哲羅的未婚妻，可是她的嫁妝都在船上隨著哥哥一起沉沒了。這不幸的女子遭受的打擊是多麼沉重呀！她哥哥對她呵護備至，可是她不但失去了這位高貴有名望的哥哥，在失去財產之後，她也失去那道貌岸然的未婚夫安哲羅的愛。他妄稱發現這位高貴女子有見不得人之事（真正的原因是她沒有了嫁妝），於是拋棄她，任她哭泣流淚，也不安慰她半點。他這樣無情無義，怎麼看她都應該對他死了心，可是就像水流遇阻，反倒愈加湍急難平，瑪莉安娜仍一如當初那樣地愛著她狠心的未婚夫。」

P. 162　　公爵更明白地說出他的計畫，即：伊莎貝拉去找安哲羅，表面上答應半夜去找他，如他所要求的一樣。這樣一來，她就可以得到特赦的承諾。然後讓瑪莉安娜代替她赴約，讓安哲羅在黑暗中把她當成伊莎貝拉。

　　「好姑娘，做這件事情毋需擔憂。」假扮的修士說：「安哲羅是她的未婚夫，讓他們這樣在一起並沒有罪。」

　　此計讓伊莎貝拉很高興，她照修士所吩咐的去做，修士則前去通知瑪莉安娜。在這之前，他就假扮成修士去探訪過這位不幸的女子，給她宗教輔導和親切慰問，並在其間從她本人口中得知了她不幸的遭遇。她現在當他是神職人員，一下子就答應聽他的指示行事。

　　見完安哲羅，伊莎貝拉便去瑪莉安娜家，公爵跟她約在那裡見面。公爵說：「妳來得正好，正是時候。那位好攝政有什麼消息？」

P. 164　　伊莎貝拉描述她安排此事的事宜。「安哲羅有一座四面都圍有磚牆的花園。」她說：「花園的西邊是一座葡萄園，進葡萄園要通過一道門。」

　　她把安哲羅交給她的兩把鑰匙拿給公爵和瑪莉安娜看，說道：「這把比較大的鑰匙是用來開葡萄園的大門，從葡萄園進入花園的小門，則是用這另一把來開。我答應他半夜會去那裡找他，而他也答應一定會饒了我弟弟一命。他輕聲低語，鬼鬼祟祟，匆匆地帶我走了兩次路，我仔細謹慎地記下那個地方。」

　　「你們有沒有設下什麼暗號，瑪莉安娜必須遵守？」公爵問。

　　「沒，沒有暗號。」伊莎貝拉回答：「只說天黑時過去。我跟他說我只能待一會兒，因為我讓他相信有一個僕人會陪我來，僕人以為我是為我弟弟的事情前來。」

P. 165　　公爵稱讚她安排得周到。她轉向瑪莉安娜，說道：「妳不需要對安哲羅說什麼，離開他時，只需低聲細語地說：『記得我弟弟的事！』」

當天晚上，伊莎貝拉帶瑪莉安娜到約定之處。伊莎貝拉很高興，心想這個辦法既能救弟弟一命，又能保住自己的貞潔。

但公爵很不放心她弟弟的性命安危，於是半夜再度造訪監獄。也幸虧他去找克勞狄，要不然克勞狄當晚就遭斬首了。因為公爵走進牢裡不久，狠心的攝政就送來一道命令，下令斬首克勞狄，並在清晨五點時把首級送到他面前。

然而公爵說服獄吏延緩對克勞狄行刑，而為了瞞過安哲羅，他勸他把凌晨一個命喪牢中者的人頭送去給他。

P. 166　但獄吏當時認為他不過是個修士而生疑，為了說服獄吏同意，公爵就拿一封公爵的親筆信給獄吏看，上面還用公爵的封印封緘。獄吏看過之後，推想修士一定帶有不在的公爵的祕令，便同意放過克勞狄，然後把那個死者的腦袋瓜砍下來，帶去給安哲羅。

之後公爵用他的真實身分寫了一封信給安哲羅，信上表示因為某些意外，他將結束旅程，隔天早上就會返抵維也納，並吩咐安哲羅在城門迎接，交還政權。公爵還命令安哲羅發出公告說，百姓凡欲控訴不公，可待他一進城門，就在街上公開申訴。

伊莎貝拉一大早來到監獄，公爵已經在那裡等她。為了保密，公爵認為告訴她克勞狄已經被斬首較為妥當。因此當伊莎貝拉問安哲羅是否已經赦免她弟弟時，他回答：「安哲羅已經處決了克勞狄，他的頭被砍下來，送去給攝政了。」

P. 168　傷心欲絕的姐姐叫喊著：「不幸的克勞狄啊，可憐的伊莎貝拉啊，害人的世界啊，好狠毒的安哲羅啊！」

　　假扮的修士請她節哀,待她平靜了一些之後,他告訴她公爵即將返回,又教她該如何控告安哲羅,並表示若案情一時不利於她,也別擔心。在充分指示過伊莎貝拉後,他又去找瑪莉安娜,告訴她該如何進行。

P. 169　　之後公爵脫下修士服,穿上自己的貴族長袍,而效忠他的民眾簇集迎接,他就在歡欣鼓舞的人潮中進入維也納城。安哲羅也在此迎接他,正式交回政權。

　　這時伊莎貝拉出現,她以申訴者的姿態投訴說:「冤枉啊!最尊貴的公爵呀!我是一個叫做克勞狄的人的姐姐,克勞狄因為誘拐一名少女,被判斬首。我請求安哲羅大人赦免我弟弟,我是怎樣下跪哀求,他是怎樣拒絕我,我又是怎樣回應他,這都說來話長,不需對您多提。我現在帶著悲痛和羞恥,要說明那可惡的結果。安哲羅要我答應他無恥的求歡,才肯放過我弟弟。我內心不斷掙扎,最後我對弟弟的憐憫勝過了我的矜持,我對他屈服了。但隔天一大清早,安哲羅就背信,下令將我不幸的弟弟斬首!」

MARIANA. My husband bids me; now I will unmask.

　　公爵佯裝不相信她的話。安哲羅表示，她弟弟依據正當的法律被處死後，她因為傷心而神智失常。

P. 170　　這時又出現了另一個投訴者：瑪莉安娜。瑪莉安娜說：「高貴的親王啊，光線來自天上，真理出自口中。真理之中有常理，道德之中有真理。仁慈的殿下啊，我是此人之妻，伊莎貝拉的話都是騙人的。她說她那晚和安哲羅在一起，事實上那晚我都和他待在花園的房子裡。我說的都是真的，請讓我起身，不然就讓我成為定於此處的大理石雕像。」

　　這時伊莎貝拉請求傳喚羅德維修士，證明她所言屬實，羅德維就是公爵喬裝時所用的假名。

P. 171　　伊莎貝拉和瑪莉安娜所言，都是依照公爵的指示。公爵打算在全維也納人民面前公開證明伊莎貝拉的清白，安哲羅萬萬想不到，正因如此，她們兩人的供詞才會不同。安哲羅想藉由兩人供詞的矛盾，把伊莎貝拉所要控告他的罪名洗刷乾淨。他裝出一副被冤枉的無辜表情，說道：

「到現在，臣都只是一笑置之，但是殿下，臣的耐心已經到達極限，臣猜想這兩個可憐的瘋女人是被利用了，幕後有個更大的黑手在指使她們。殿下，就讓臣來調查這樁陰謀吧。」

「好，我非常贊成。」公爵說：「你高興怎麼處置她們，就怎麼處置她們。你，艾斯卡大臣，你陪他一道審問，全力支援他去查究這宗誹謗案。我已經下令傳喚指使她們的修士了，修士來了以後，你可以依你所蒙受的損失，給他應有的懲罰。我要離開你們一會兒，但安哲羅大臣，在未完全判決好這宗誹謗案之前，你不可以離開。」

P. 172　　公爵說完就離開。安哲羅很滿意能夠擔任代理法官，做自己這樁案件的仲裁人。

公爵稍作離開，卸下貴族長袍，穿上修士服。喬裝好之後，他又回到安哲羅和艾斯卡面前。好心的老艾斯卡以為安哲羅遭到誣告，就對喬裝的修士說：「先生，你有指使這兩位女子誹謗安哲羅大臣嗎？」

修士回答：「公爵在哪裡？應該是他來聽證的。」

艾斯卡回答：「我們就代表公爵來聽證，你實話實說。」

「至少我會放膽地說。」修士回嘴道。他指責公爵不該把伊莎貝拉的控訴案交給她所要控訴的人，又不諱言說他是維也納城的一個旁觀者，看到了很多腐敗的事。艾斯卡揚言，他的言論反叛政府，指謫公爵的操守，要受酷刑，打入牢裡。這時假扮的修士卸下偽裝，眾人認出是公爵本人，莫不吃驚，安哲羅尤其驚慌。

P. 173　　公爵先對伊莎貝拉說：「伊莎貝拉，妳過來。妳的修士現在是妳的親王了，我換了衣服，可是我的心並沒有變，仍衷心為你服務。」

「啊，請饒恕我。」
伊莎貝拉說：「小民不知
情，竟然勞煩了殿下。」

他表示，他未能制
止她弟弟的死刑，才真
需要她原諒。為了進一
步考驗她的品德，他目
前還不想告訴她克勞狄
還活著。

安哲羅如今知曉公
爵暗中親眼看到他所做
的勾當，便說：「啊，威
嚴的殿下，見到殿下的
本領非凡，知悉臣的行
為，臣若想再掩飾，就
是罪加一等。請英明的殿下莫讓臣再羞慚下去，就把臣的招供
當作是問罪，只求殿下隆恩，立刻賜臣一死。」

P. 174　　公爵回答：「安哲羅，你罪證確鑿，我們就送你上克勞狄
彎腰受刑的斷頭臺上，同樣速速行刑。至於他的財產，瑪莉安
娜，我們要判給妳。名義上妳是他的寡婦，妳可以用這筆財產
去找一個更好的丈夫。」

「啊，仁慈的殿下！」瑪莉安娜說：「我不要別人，也不要
更好的男人。」說著她跪下來，就像伊莎貝拉請求饒恕克勞狄
一命那樣，這個賢妻為不知圖報的丈夫安哲羅求饒性命。她
說：「仁慈的君王，啊，好殿下呀！好心的伊莎貝拉，幫幫我
吧！跟我一起下跪求情，我願終生效犬馬之勞！」

　　公爵說：「妳求她是很不合情理的，要是伊莎貝拉也下跪懇求開恩，她弟弟的鬼魂就要破墓而出，含恨地帶走她了。」

　　但瑪莉安娜仍說：「伊莎貝拉，好心的伊莎貝拉，妳只要跪在我旁邊，舉起手，不用說話，一切由我來說就行了！大家都說，至善者是由錯誤中鍛鍊而來的，大部分的人都因犯了些過失而變得更好，我的丈夫也可能如此。哦，伊莎貝拉！妳跟我一起下跪好嗎？」

P. 176　　公爵說：「他要償克勞狄一命。」

　　可是當伊莎貝拉也在他面前跪下時，好心的公爵心下甚喜，他始終期盼她行事仁厚正直。伊莎貝拉說：「慈恩浩蕩的君王，若殿下願意，就把這個被判死刑的人當作是我還活著的弟弟吧。在他遇見我之前，我諒他所作所為還算忠於職責。既然如此，且饒他一命吧！我弟弟只是接受法治，觸法而死。」

　　看到這位高貴的求情者為仇人性命說情，公爵的最佳回應就是：派人把仍以為自己命運未卜的克勞狄從牢裡帶出來，把他活生生地交給為他哀悼的伊莎貝拉。公爵對伊莎貝拉說：「伊莎貝拉，把手給我。看在妳這可愛人兒的分上，我赦免了克勞狄。若妳願意嫁給我，那他也就是我的弟弟了。」

　　安哲羅大臣一時之間感到自己已經安全無虞，公爵看到他的眼睛隱約為之一亮，就說道：「好了，安哲羅，你可得疼愛你的夫人，是她的美德讓你得到赦免的。瑪莉安娜，恭喜妳了！安哲羅，好好愛她！我聽過她的告白，知道她的美德。」

P. 177　　安哲羅想起自己在代理職權的那段短短時間裡，是如何的鐵石心腸。如今，他才嚐到慈悲的滋味是如何甜美。

　　公爵命令克勞狄迎娶茱麗葉，自己則又再一次向伊莎貝拉求婚。她的美德和高貴的情操，讓她贏得親王的愛。

　　伊莎貝拉尚未正式成為修女，可以結婚。高貴的公爵偽裝成卑微的修士時，曾經好心地幫助過她，她於是欣然感恩地接受了他給予的光榮。伊莎貝拉成為維也納的公爵夫人後，她的高尚品德樹立了的良好典範，全城的年輕姑娘從此完全變了個樣，再也沒有人像茱麗葉那樣越矩。而今，後悔的茱麗葉，也成為那改過自新的克勞狄之妻了。寬厚仁慈的公爵和他鍾愛的伊莎貝拉統治了好些年，他是最幸福的丈夫和親王了。

冬天的故事

P. 192　　西西里國王雷提斯和德貌雙全的王后荷麥妮，有過一段琴瑟和鳴的日子。擁有這麼出色的夫人，雷提斯萬般幸福，一切稱心如意，只是有時懸念再見到波希米亞國王波利茲這位老同窗，也好讓他認識認識自己的皇后。

　　雷提斯和波利茲兩人穿著同一條開襠褲長大，可惜在他們父王死後，就各自被召回去統治王國。雖然雙方常交流貢品、信函和大使，但兩人已經好幾年沒見過面了。

　　最後，在一再的邀請之下，波利茲終於從波希米亞來到西西里宮廷拜訪好友雷提斯。

P. 194　　一開始，這件事讓雷提斯雀躍不已。他請王后要特別招待他這位兒時同伴，能和死黨老友相聚首，他感到非常興奮。他們聊起舊日時光，回憶學生時代和年輕時玩過的把戲，並說給始終興致昂昂在旁聆聽的皇后荷麥妮聽。

　　住了好一陣子之後，波利茲準備啟程告辭，雷提斯要荷麥妮和他一塊請

波利茲再多留幾天。

　　未料這件事竟成為好皇后傷心的肇端，因為波利茲原本拒絕雷提斯，卻被她的溫柔勸說給打動，決定留下來多待幾個星期。

　　儘管雷提斯熟知好友波利茲為人正直，行事光明磊落，也明白賢德王后的品行絕佳，卻仍起了無可遏止的嫉妒心。

P. 196　　荷麥妮按丈夫的要求善待波利茲，為的只是討丈夫歡心，未料卻反而讓這可悲的國王更加妒火中燒。國王原本是位熱情忠貞的朋友，也是個最好、最溫柔的丈夫，卻在轉眼間變成一頭凶猛蠻橫的怪物。他召來宮裡的勛爵卡密羅，跟他說心裡頭的疑忌，要他去把波利茲毒死。

　　卡密羅心眼好，他很清楚雷提斯根本只是在亂吃飛醋，所以不但沒有下毒加害波利茲，還把國王主子的命令告訴了他，然後同意和他一起逃出西西里國境。在卡密羅的幫助下，波利茲安全回到自己的波希米亞王國。此後，卡密羅就留在這位國王的宮廷裡，成為波利茲的至交和愛臣。

　　波利茲一逃走，嫉妒的雷提斯更加憤怒。他跑去皇后的寢宮，看見善良的夫人和小兒子馬密利並肩而坐，馬密利正準備講他最得意的故事來讓母親開心。未料國王一進來，就把孩子帶走，兀自將荷麥妮打入大牢。

P. 198　　年幼的馬密利摯愛著母親，他看到她受到這樣侮辱，被人從他身旁給拉進牢裡，好不傷心。他漸漸消沉，日形憔悴，食不下嚥，夜不成眠，恐將悲傷而死。

　　把皇后關進牢裡後，國王派了克里歐和迪翁這兩名西西里勛爵，到德爾菲的阿波羅神廟求神諭，想知道皇后是否對他不忠。

P. 199　　進了牢裡沒多久，荷麥妮生下一女。看著可愛的嬰兒，可憐的夫人感到安慰多了。她對孩子說：「我可憐的小囚犯，我和你一樣無辜啊！」

　　荷麥妮有個性格高尚的好友寶琳娜，寶琳娜是西西里勛爵安提貢的妻子，她一聽說皇后生子，就前去荷麥妮受禁的地牢，對服侍荷麥妮的愛蜜莉說：「愛蜜莉，請你去跟皇后說，如果她信得過我，我就帶嬰兒到她父王那邊，說不定他看了這無辜的孩子就會心軟了。」

　　愛蜜莉回答：「可敬的夫人呀，我會跟皇后說這個好主意的，她今天還希望有朋友敢把小孩帶給國王。」

　　寶琳娜說：「妳跟她說，我會為她跟雷提斯辯解求情的。」

P. 200　　「妳對慈愛的皇后這麼好，願上帝永遠保佑妳啊！」

　　愛蜜莉說完，立刻去找荷麥妮。荷麥妮興奮地把嬰兒交給寶琳娜，她還擔心沒有人敢把小孩帶給國王呢！

　　寶琳娜抱著這個初生的小嬰兒要去見國王，她丈夫害怕她會激怒國王，便一路阻擋她。然而她硬是闖到國王面前，把小孩放在國王腳邊，然後義正嚴詞地為荷麥妮辯護。她痛斥國王沒人性，懇求他放過這對無辜的母女。

　　但寶琳娜激昂的諫言只是惹得雷提斯更加不悅，便命令她丈夫安提貢把她帶下去。

　　寶琳娜把小嬰兒留在嬰兒父親的腳邊，逕自離開。她想，等他們一獨處，他看過孩子之後，就會為她的清白無辜動容了。

P. 202　　只可惜好心的寶琳娜估錯算盤。她人才一離開，這位狠心的父親就要她丈夫安提貢把孩子帶出海，扔到無人的岸上，讓她自生自滅。

　　安提貢不比好心腸的卡密羅。他對雷提斯言聽計從，立刻就搭船帶孩子出海，準備一遇見荒岸，就把她扔下。

　　國王一味認定荷麥妮對他不忠，也不等去德爾菲的阿波羅廟求神諭的克里歐和迪翁回來，在皇后產後身子尚虛，還在為失去寶貝女兒而傷心之際，就把她押到朝廷上，當著朝臣貴族的面前公開審判她。

P. 203　　國內眾大臣、法官和貴族都齊聚來審判荷麥妮，這位憂悒的皇后囚犯站在眾人面前，等待判決。就在這時，克里歐和迪翁走進議會，把密封的神諭結果上呈國王。雷提斯命人拆封，將神諭大聲讀出來。神諭上寫著：

> 荷麥妮清清白白，
> 波利茲無可指責，
> 卡密羅一介忠臣，
> 雷提斯善妒暴君。
> 若不尋回被棄者，
> 國王身後無可繼。

P. 204　怎奈國王就是不相信這則神諭。他說這是皇后的親信所編造出來的，要法官繼續審問皇后。雷提斯話猶未了，但見一人走進來稟告說，馬密利王子因為聽到母親要被判死罪，竟悲傷和羞恥到暴斃了。

　　一聽到這個情深的愛子為自己的不幸傷心而亡，荷麥妮暈厥了過去。這個消息也讓雷提斯萬分錐心，開始對不幸的皇后起了憐憫心。他命令寶琳娜和皇后的宮女們把皇后帶下去，想辦法讓她清醒。

　　一會兒後，寶琳娜回來稟報國王，說荷麥妮已經香消玉殞。

　　聽到皇后的噩耗，雷提斯這才悔恨自己對她太狠心，心想自己對她的虐待一定傷透了她的心。他現在相信了她的清白，也相信神諭所言屬實。他想，神諭上所言的「若不尋回被棄者」，指的應該就是他的小女兒，畢竟小王子馬密利已經不在人間，他沒有其他子嗣了。現在，他倒願意用他的王國來換回被棄的女兒。他自責不已，在悲傷悔恨中度過了許多年。

P.205　　安提貢帶著尚在襁褓中的公主搭船出海，因為一場暴風雨，船隻被吹到波希米亞境內的海岸上，那裡正是正直國王波利茲的王國。上岸後，安提貢扔下小嬰兒後逕自離去。

　　結果，安提貢再也沒有回到西西里向雷提斯稟告公主被棄的地點，因為當他要返回船上時，林子裡跑出一隻熊，把他撕個稀爛。他依雷提斯那個沒天良的命令行事，這是他應得的懲罰。

P.206　　荷麥妮要讓小女兒去見雷提斯時，精心為她穿戴了華服寶飾。安提貢則在她的斗篷上別上一張紙，寫著「帕蒂坦」這個名字，還有幾句暗示她出身高貴和遭遇不幸的話。

　　這名可憐的棄嬰後來被一個牧羊人發現。牧羊人心腸好，把小帕蒂坦帶回家讓老婆悉心養育。他人窮，不想讓別人知道他撿到珠寶，就搬離原本居住的地方，以免被人知道他是在哪兒發了財。他拿了帕蒂坦的一些珠寶去買了羊，成為一名有錢的牧羊人。

　　他把帕蒂坦視如己出地撫養長大，帕蒂坦也一直認為自己就是牧羊人的女兒。

　　小帕蒂坦出落得亭亭玉立。她所受的教養是一般牧羊人家給女兒的教養，但璞玉未琢的她，畢竟有母后高貴天性的遺傳。她的舉止儀態，會讓人以為她根本就是在親生父親的皇宮裡長大的。

P.209　　波希米亞國王波利茲有個獨子，叫做弗羅瑞。一次，這位年輕王子在牧羊人家附近打獵時，瞥見了這位老牧羊人所謂的女兒。帕蒂坦的美麗、靦腆和尊貴的氣質，霎時讓他一見鐘情。

不久王子假扮成平民，取名多里克，常跑去老牧羊人家逗留。波利茲發現弗羅瑞常常不在宮中，便派人監督他兒子，結果得知弗羅瑞原來是迷戀上牧羊人的美麗女兒。

波利茲召來曾把他從雷提斯手中救出來的忠臣卡密羅，要卡密羅陪他去找帕蒂坦的牧羊人父親。

喬裝過的波利茲和卡密羅來到老牧羊人的家裡時，人們正在舉行剪羊毛儀式。因逢盛會，他們這兩個陌生人受到歡迎，被邀請進屋，參加慶典活動。

P. 210　整個活動好不歡樂。人們擺好桌子，備好上等酒菜，慶祝農家盛宴。有些少男、少女在屋前的綠地上歡舞，有些年輕人在門口跟小販買絲帶、手套等這類的小玩意兒。

P. 211　在這熱鬧的氣氛中，弗羅瑞和帕蒂坦卻獨自坐在一旁的角落裡。與其加入周圍鬧哄哄的娛樂活動，他們似乎更喜歡和彼此聊天談心。

國王經過喬裝，兒子認不出他，他便趁機走近兩人，偷聽他們談話。看到和兒子說話的帕蒂坦單純又優雅，波利茲很是訝異。他對卡密羅說：「我從沒見過這麼漂亮而出身低下的姑娘，她說話和表現出來的樣子都不像是這種出身的人，她的高貴和這個地方一點也不相稱呀。」

卡密羅答道：「的確，她可說是牧羊人之后啊！」

「請問你，好心的朋友。」國王問老牧羊人說：「正在跟你女兒講話的俊俏年輕人是誰呀？」

P. 212　牧羊人回答：「他叫多里克。他說他愛上我女兒，但老實說，你看他們兩人親嘴的樣子，誰也不會愛得比誰少啊！多里克這孩子要是真能娶到她，她會帶給他意想不到的福氣呢！」老牧人指的是帕蒂坦剩下的珠寶。他拿一些珠寶來買羊群，剩下的珠寶他就小心保管，想給她當嫁妝。

P. 213　波利茲接著對兒子說：「小伙子，現在是怎麼回事？」他說：「你的魂好像被攝走了，無心參加宴會。我年輕的時候，常常送禮物給情人，而你竟然那樣就讓小販走了，也不給你的情人買些什麼。」

年輕的王子完全沒料到跟他說話的是父王。他答道：「老先生，帕蒂坦不在乎這些小玩意的，她想要的禮物是鎖在我心頭裡的東西。」

他說罷，便轉向帕蒂坦，說道：「帕蒂坦，這位老先生想必也曾是個多情人。現在當著他的面，請妳聽我的告白吧，也讓他聽聽我是怎麼說的。」

　　弗羅瑞要向帕蒂坦鄭重求婚，他請這個陌生老翁作證人。他對波利茲說：「請您為我們證婚。」

　　「我看是為你們的分手作證，小伙子。」國王表明真實身分。

P. 215　　波利茲斥責兒子竟敢和出身卑微的女孩訂婚，又用「羊崽子」、「羊鉤子」等輕蔑的稱呼來叫帕蒂坦，還威脅她要是再跟他兒子見面，就要把她和她的老牧羊人父親處死。

　　國王說完後，氣沖沖地離開，命令卡密羅帶王子弗羅瑞隨後跟上。

　　國王的責罵倒是凸顯了帕蒂坦高貴的本性，他離開後，帕蒂坦說：「雖然我們的關係完了，但我不怕。剛剛我有一兩次都很想插話，很想明白地告訴他，照耀他皇宮的太陽，同樣也照耀我們的小茅屋，它可是一視同仁的。」

　　她接著悲傷地說：「但現在我是大夢初醒了，我再也不會自詡為女王了。先生，你走吧，我要去擠羊奶，然後邊掉淚。」

P. 217　　好心腸的卡密羅深深地被帕蒂坦的特質和得體的舉止所吸引，而且他也看出來，深愛她的年輕王子是不會為了父命而離棄她。這時他心生良策，不但可以幫助這對情侶，還可以實現他心裡盼想的計畫呢。

　　卡密羅早就知道西西里國王雷提斯已經真心悔過，儘管他現在是波利茲國王的至交，他仍渴望再見到以前服侍過的國王和故鄉。他建議弗羅瑞和帕蒂坦跟他一起回西西里宮廷，並擔保雷提斯會保護他們，由雷提斯出面調解，直到波利茲寬恕他們並答應婚事。

　　他們很高興地接受了這個建議。卡密羅安排潛逃的一切事宜，並答應讓老牧羊人和他們一起上路。

P. 219　　老牧羊人隨身帶上帕蒂坦剩下的珠寶，還有嬰兒裝和別在斗篷上的紙條。

　　他們沿途平順，弗羅瑞、帕蒂坦、卡密羅和老牧羊人一行人，最後平安地來到雷提斯的宮殿。此時雷提斯仍為死去的荷麥妮和棄子哀傷。他殷勤接待卡密羅，也熱誠歡迎弗羅瑞王子。

　　然而當弗羅瑞以王妃的身分介紹帕蒂坦時，他看得目瞪口呆，帕蒂坦和死去的荷麥妮長得如此相似，讓他不禁悲從中來。

他說，如果當初沒有狠心殺掉女兒，那女兒現在也是這樣一位可愛的姑娘了。

他對弗羅瑞說：「而且，我還和你賢明的父親斷絕來往，失去彼此的友誼。現在，只要能再見到他，我死也甘願。」

P. 220 國王這麼注意帕蒂坦，又說曾失去一個在襁褓裡就被丟棄的女兒，老牧羊人於是推算他撿到小帕蒂坦的時間，再推想她遭棄時的樣子，還有其他象徵貴族出身的珠寶等等，最後他不得不推論出：帕蒂坦就是國王的女兒。

老牧羊人向國王稟奏他撿到孩子的經過，弗羅瑞、帕蒂坦、卡密羅和忠誠的寶琳娜都在旁聆聽。他還描述了安提貢遇難時的情況，說他目睹了熊撲在安提貢的身上。

之後他拿出一件華麗的斗篷，寶琳娜認出來那就是荷麥妮用來包裹孩子的斗篷。他又拿出一件珠寶，她也記得荷麥妮曾將它掛在帕蒂坦的頸子上。最後他拿出紙條，寶琳娜認出那是丈夫的筆跡。這一下子，帕蒂坦無疑就是雷提斯的親生女兒。但是，唉！寶琳娜內心裡衝突不已，她既為丈夫的死而悲傷，又為神諭的應驗而高興：這下子國王終於找回繼承人，找回他當初遺棄的女兒了。

P. 221 聽到帕蒂坦就是自己的女兒，又想到過世的荷麥妮看不到親生孩子，雷提斯悲慟得久久不能言語，只說出：「啊！妳的母親，妳的母親！」

P. 222 在這悲喜交集之際，寶琳娜插話對雷提斯說，她有座雕像，最近才剛由優異的義大利大師朱利諾・羅馬諾所完成。那座雕像和皇后維妙維肖，要是國王陛下肯去她家瞧瞧，一定也會以為那就是荷麥妮本人。於是眾人便出發前往她家，國王迫不及待想看長得和荷麥妮一模一樣的雕像，帕蒂坦也渴望知道未曾謀面的母親的樣子。

寶琳娜把遮蓋美麗雕像的帷幕拉開。看到雕像和荷麥妮如此神似，國王的悲傷全湧了上來，好一段時間都說不出話，只是木然不動。

「國王陛下，看您一語不發，我倒高興，這表示您真的很驚訝。您看，這雕像是不是很像皇后？」寶琳娜說。

國王終於開口道：「啊，我當初向她求婚時，她就是站這個樣子的，是這樣的雍容華貴。可是寶琳娜，妳看，雕像看起來比荷麥妮老呀！」

P. 223 寶琳娜答道：「這正是雕刻師傅厲害的地方，

他把雕像雕得栩栩如生。陛下，我要把帷幕放下了，免得您等一下還以為它會動。」

P. 224　　國王說：「不要把帷幕放下，除非我死了！卡密羅，你看，你不覺得她好像會呼吸嗎？她的眼睛好像在動呢！」

　　「國王陛下，我真的要把帷幕放下了啦！」寶琳娜說：「您看得太出神了，會誤以為雕像是活的。」

P. 225　　「啊，親愛的寶琳娜。」雷提斯說：「那就讓我接下來的二十年都這麼想吧！我仍能感覺到她的氣息。有什麼鬼斧神工可以連呼吸都刻得出來呢？誰都不准笑我，我要去親吻她。」

　　「啊！我的好陛下！那不成啊！」寶琳娜說：「雕像嘴唇上的紅漆還沒乾，您的唇會沾上油彩的。我可以把帷幕放下了嗎？」

「不行，二十年之內都不准放下。」雷提斯說。

始終跪在一旁的帕蒂坦，靜靜仰望著完美無瑕的母親雕像。她說：「我也可以在這裡待上二十年，一直望著我親愛的母親。」

「你們兩個都不要再胡思亂想了。」寶琳娜對雷提斯說：「讓我把帷幕放下，免得您還會更吃驚。我可以讓雕像移動，叫它從座台上走下來，牽您的手。不過您一定會以為是什麼妖術在幫我，我先聲明我可沒有。」

P. 226 國王驚訝地說：「不管妳叫它做什麼，我都很想看。如果妳讓她說話，我也很想聽。妳要是能讓她動，也就能讓她講話吧。」

　　寶琳娜命人奏起預先就準備好的莊嚴慢樂。只見眾人驚訝
不已，因為雕像竟從座台上走了下來。它用手臂摟住雷提斯的
脖子，並說話來為丈夫和剛剛找回的孩子帕蒂坦祈願祝福。

　　難怪雕像會摟著雷提斯的脖子，會保祐丈夫和孩子。也難
怪呀，因為這座雕像就是荷麥妮本人，是如假包換、活生生的
皇后。

　　寶琳娜向國王謊報荷麥妮的死訊，是因為心想只有這個辦
法可以保住皇后的性命。此後，荷麥妮就住在好心的寶琳娜那
裡。要不是聽說已經找到帕蒂坦，荷麥妮也不會讓雷提斯知道
她還活著。雖然她早就原諒雷提斯帶給她的傷害，卻無法原諒
他那樣狠心對待襁褓中的女兒。

P. 227　　死去的皇后復活，被棄的女兒尋回，悲傷已久的雷提斯欣
喜欲狂。

各方無不捎來祝賀和熱切的問候。這對父母開心地感謝弗羅瑞王子對女兒的愛，她一度只是出身卑微的女孩。他們也祝福好心的老牧羊人，他搭救扶養了他們的孩子。卡密羅和寶琳娜也好不歡喜，可以親眼看到自己的盡忠效力得到了這樣的好結局。

P. 228　　這時，像是為了使這奇異意外的喜悅更加圓滿似的，波利茲國王也來到了皇宮。

　　卡密羅早就渴望歸鄉，當初兒子和卡密羅失蹤時，波利茲就料想可以在西西里找到這兩個人。他全速追趕他們，剛好在雷提斯一生最快樂的時刻裡趕到。

P. 229　　波利茲與大家同樂，他原諒好友雷提斯對他亂吃飛醋，兩人再度重修舊好，就像小時候那樣相親相愛。現在再也不用擔心波利茲會反對兒子娶帕蒂坦了，帕蒂坦也不再是什麼羊鉤子，而是西西里的皇位繼承人了。

　　我們看到具有堅忍德性的荷麥妮，長年受苦之後終於得到回報。這個完美的女性和雷提斯及帕蒂坦一起過了好多年，這一下她可是最幸福的母親和皇后了。

ÆTATIS · SVÆ · 47 ·

A⁰

· A : 1612 ·

悅讀
莎士比亞
經典喜劇故事

馴悍記
終成眷屬
一報還一報
冬天的故事

作者 _ Charles and Mary Lamb
前言／導讀 _ 陳敬旻
譯者 _ Cosmos Language Workshop
編輯 _ 安卡斯
校對 _ 陳慧莉
封面設計 _ 林書玉
製程管理 _ 洪巧玲
發行人 _ 周均亮
出版者 _ 寂天文化事業股份有限公司
電話 _ +886-2-2365-9739
傳真 _ +886-2-2365-9835
網址 _ www.icosmos.com.tw
讀者服務 _ onlineservice@icosmos.com.tw
出版日期 _ 2018年12月 初版一刷（250101）
郵撥帳號 _ 1998620-0 寂天文化事業股份有限公司

國家圖書館出版品預行編目資料

悅讀莎士比亞經典喜劇故事 / Charles and Mary
Lamb 著；Cosmos Language Workshop 譯；
—初版. —[臺北市]：寂天文化, 2018.12 面；
公分. 中英對照

ISBN　978-986-318-744-8（25K平裝附光碟片）
　　　1. 英語　2. 讀本

805.18　　　　　　　　　　　107017184